A Material World Tale

DENIM

K. C. WELLS

Acknowledgments

A huge thank you, as always, to my wonderful team of betas – Jason, Daniel, Helena, Debra, Sharon, Mardee and Will.

But a special Thank You to Daniel Parry, who was there from the first plotting meeting to the last sex scene. You rock!

K.C. WELLS

Chapter One

Harry Forrest took a drink of coffee from his insulated mug and stared out at the passing scenery. Not that Croydon was all that scenic to start with. The houses blurred into one another and the traffic was reduced to a hum that he tried to blot out as the bus edged closer and closer to the recruitment office where he worked.

Harry wasn't thinking about work. He was already focused on the weekend. Wednesday was definitely hump day, and there was the pub quiz to look forward to on Friday. But after that, the weekend would take its usual course, just like every other weekend for the past God knew many years. Saturday night would be spent watching Strictly Come Dancing, just Harry, a couple of cans of lager, and a large packet of Kettle chips. Then there was the ritual cleaning fest, not to mention the joy of the weekly shopping trip to Tesco's. He'd spend the rest of the weekend trying not to notice the fading wallpaper that badly needed replacing, the white woodwork that wasn't white any longer, the kitchen cabinets that screamed 1970s...

The whole house was stuck in that decade, had been ever since his Dad had bought it. Mum had been gone for three years, and Harry still hadn't gotten around to doing a single thing to change the decor. Just like his wardrobe, really. He wore the same suits to work, the same pair of worn, faded sweatpants and baggy tops when he was at home.

Why change? There was no one to dress for, right?

There were times when he felt a damn sight older than thirty-five. There were other occasions when that thought filled him with self-loathing. He saw his life, saw the monotony of it all, and yet felt helpless to step off the escalator that took him further and further down.

What I need is a change of direction. If he could find the motivation.

With a start, Harry realized it was his stop next. He closed the lid on his mug, grabbed his bag, and lurched towards the steep stairs that led to the lower deck. Deb was already there, hanging onto the bar. She appeared pleased to see him.

"I didn't know you were on this one. I'd 'ave come upstairs an' sat with you otherwise."

Harry was secretly glad she hadn't. He preferred his morning bus trip to be quiet, while he steeled himself for the coming day. Deb was okay though, always with a cheerful smile and a kind word for everyone. He was really lucky when it came to the staff in his office. They were a good bunch of colleagues.

The bus shuddered to a halt, and they were the only two passengers to descend. They walked slowly along the road, past the construction site where cement mixers were already turning. Harry spotted two or three guys on the scaffolding, carrying girders, hammering, all busy, despite the early hour.

I guess that's why they're always long gone when I get out of work. Early start, early finish. Harry envied them. It showed every sign of being a gorgeous day to be outdoors. Spring had long since morphed into summer, and the temperature was pleasant.

A loud wolf whistle ripped through the air, and Deb turned to stare at the workman. She blew him a kiss, then glanced at Harry. "Well, that made my day."

Harry chuckled. "You're in there," he joked.

Her eyes held a wicked gleam. "Oh yeah. I could do with a nice bit of rough. Love a guy who's good with 'is 'ands."

The words were right there on the tip of Harry's tongue. *Don't we all?*

Another saucy whistle blasted the air, and she giggled. "I think you're right. I wonder if he'll still be around when I get out of work." Deb grinned. "I could ask him back to my place for a massage. I'm sure that's just what he'll need after a hard day's grafting—a good rub-down."

"Subtle, Deb, really subtle." Harry didn't bother looking in the direction of the whistler. It wasn't as if *he'd* be the object of anyone's attention.

Deb laughed. "Listen, life's too short to waste opportunities that come your way. My old dad used to say, you always regret *not* doing something. And if I get the chance to bounce on *that* gorgeous hunk, I'm not gonna say no, right?"

Harry was glad he wasn't drinking his coffee right then. "Christ, Deb. I think that comes under the heading of TMI." It wasn't an image he particularly wanted in his head.

Deb snickered. "Don't tell me you don't have the same thoughts. I've seen your screen saver, remember."

That did it. As soon as he reached his desk, Harry was going to get rid of the Antonio Banderas wallpaper, and replace it with something innocuous, like fluffy kittens or puppies or bunnies.

Thankfully, Deb fell silent for the last five minutes of their walk, and they passed through the door of the office, the first to arrive. Another day loomed in front of him, and for a moment, Harry envied Deb. He could remember being on the receiving end of wolf whistles, but that had been a long time ago, when Harry had been a good deal slimmer, a frequenter of London's gay clubs and bars.

A long time ago? It felt like a lifetime.

Harry shut down his computer with a sigh of contentment. Time to go home to a long shower, a Chicken Tikka Masala, and Eastenders. Around him was the chatter of the ten or so staff who worked in the recruitment office, all equally glad to be going home.

Harry cleared his throat. "Folks? Don't forget this Friday is Pub Quiz night at the Red Lion. This month's charity is the local hospice, so let's have a good turnout. If you haven't signed up yet to be on the team, the list is on the staff noticeboard." He'd taken a look earlier, and there had only been two names on it. They normally managed five or six people.

"And remember it's also Lou's last day," Sally added. "So even if you don't want to be on the team, you can still come along, support those who are, and buy Lou a drink."

Lou coughed. "Only, if you lot get me too

drunk, you're paying for my taxi ride home."
Laughter followed her words. Lou had been with
them for three years, a popular lady whose daughter
was about to give birth to her first child.
Unfortunately, she lived in Australia, and had asked
her mother to stay with them for a couple of months.
Lou had been counting down the days.

"Are you packed yet?" Deb asked, pulling on
her jacket.

Lou snorted. "We've been packed for the last
month. And my other half won't thank you if I get
on that flight Saturday morning with a hangover."
She glanced at Deb. "What's got you in such a hurry
this evening? You're usually one of the last to
leave."

Harry couldn't restrain his smirk. "She's
hoping to catch someone."

Deb narrowed her gaze but said nothing. "I'll
see you all tomorrow. Have a good night."

"You too." Harry kept his face straight. As
she passed his desk, he couldn't help adding, "Good
luck" under his breath. Not that he would be all that
far behind her, judging by the speed with which
everyone was vacating the building. Harry grabbed
his cleaned mug, shoved it into his bag, and with one
last glance at the office, switched off the lights and
locked the door. The alarm activated, he turned right
and headed toward the bus stop. Ahead of him, he
spotted Deb, walking alone. As Harry neared the
construction site, he soon saw the reason why. The
site was quiet, all its workmen gone for the day.

The first thought to flash through his mind
was *Poor Deb*. Doubtless there'd be another
opportunity—it would be months before the building
would be completed. Besides, Deb was always

regaling her co-workers with tales of her dates, disastrous or otherwise.

Harry couldn't remember the last time he'd gone on a date, and he couldn't see one taking place in the foreseeable future. He ambled to the bus stop, his Oyster card ready, in no real hurry to get home to his ready meal and the TV. Then he realized he'd forgotten to mention he'd be late into work the following day. Damn. He'd have to call Sally: she had the spare set of keys.

A dentist appointment. Oh, joy.

Any more excitement and he'd probably spontaneously combust.

Harry got off the bus, his jaw starting to ache as the numbing effects of the local anaesthetic wore off. He hated fillings, and that one had snuck up on him. Still, the weekend was that little bit closer, and mundane as it certainly promised to be, it was better than being in work. He began making a shopping list in his head, mentally picturing the contents of his fridge and cupboards.

Then he stopped himself. *Wow. Shopping lists. I may die from the excitement.*

A loud wolf whistle rent the air, and Harry glanced around him. He was the only person in the street. Harry kept his head low and carried on walking. When it happened again, he came to a halt and peered toward the building site. As usual, several guys were visible, all of them busy—except one.

DENIM

A guy stood on the platform about twenty feet away, leaning on the railing. He was dressed in jeans, his chest bare, revealing an expanse of tanned skin. A metallic chain of some sort around his neck caught the sun's rays. Short, black hair glinted in the sunlight. Even from a distance, Harry could tell he was tall. And he was grinning—at Harry. Before Harry could walk on, the guy brought his fingers to his lips and let out another long, sexy whistle.

At Harry.

He didn't know what to make of it. When was the last time any guy had whistled at him? In his early twenties, sure, walking through Soho, past all the gay bars and clubs that he hadn't been anywhere near in at least six or seven years. But now? There could only be one answer.

The guy had to be in severe need of glasses.

Harry averted his gaze and picked up his speed, his aching jaw forgotten. By the time he got inside the office door, he was already telling himself that someone had made a mistake.

Deb gazed inquiringly at him as he approached his desk. "How was the dentist?"

From behind her, Sally snorted. "Since when is going to the dentist ever a good thing?" She gave Harry a reassuring smile. "Everything like clockwork this morning, Harry. I'll bring you a cup of coffee. The heat might help."

Deb waited until Sally was out of earshot, before leaning over Harry's desk and lowering her voice. "And I'm definitely losing my touch. I didn't get one bleedin' whistle from that load of gits at the building site this morning."

Harry arched his eyebrows. "Isn't that a little strong?" For the first time, it occurred to him that the previous day's attentions had not been for Deb, but then he brushed the thought aside.

Deb huffed. "If I can't pull a randy builder, I've really lost it." Then her eyes twinkled. "I'd better make sure I'm wearing my fuck-me heels and lucky knickers tomorrow night." She walked away from Harry's desk, chuckling.

Harry gazed after her fondly. Deb had been divorced for two years now, and was forever complaining that the well of gorgeous, available men that had been so prevalent before she got married, seemed to have dried up completely.

I know exactly how she feels.

Only, how was he supposed to find a gorgeous, available guy when he wouldn't get off his fat arse and make an effort? It wasn't as if such a specimen was about to come knocking on his door, right?

Then the usual gloom descended. *Who am I kidding? Who would want me?* Harry smiled to himself. Except the nearly blind guy in sexy-as-fuck jeans, of course.

Yeah, right.

Chapter Two

Harry was doing his best not to stare at the guy in the corner. It had to be the same guy, the one who'd whistled at him again from the building site that morning. He was dressed in jeans, a V-neck white T-shirt, and a denim jacket. Heavy black boots completed the look. He sat alone, a pint glass in front of him, long legs stretched out, crossed at the ankles, thumbs hooked in the waistband of those tight jeans. Lord, they were tight...

Of course, it didn't help matters that every time Harry glanced in Denim Guy's direction, he found a pair of dark eyes gazing back at him. Seriously sexy eyes.

Fuck.

Harry did his best to push the sexy-as-fuck guy from his mind, because hello? Pub quiz? His office team wasn't doing so well so far, and they'd already gone through three rounds. Thank God there was a break coming up. Harry needed a drink.

A microphone whined into life. "Okay, folks, you've got half an hour, then we'll carry on with Round Four." Carol grinned. "And it's the Photo round. You know how much you all love that." A chorus of laughter broke out. It was the most hotly debated round of the quiz, and there were always arguments.

Harry got to his feet. "I'll go get the drinks in. What are you all having?" After he'd mentally stored the five drinks requests, he strolled over to the bar, deliberately not glancing in Denim Guy's direction. With any luck, he'd already left.

"Hey there, sexy."

No such luck.

Harry took a deep breath and turned to look at the man standing next to him. Thirty-ish, black hair, cut very short, a pair of deep brown eyes, laughter lines around them, a tanned face…

Denim Guy was even better looking up close.

Harry coughed. "Do I know you?" Like Harry was going to admit he'd recognized him.

The skin around the guy's eyes crinkled with good humour. "Is that how you want to play it? Fine. I see you walk past the site every morning. You totally ignore me every time I whistle. What's it gonna take for you to come out for a drink with me?"

Harry blinked. "Me?"

"Yes, you."

"But… how do you know I'm even interested in men?"

The guy gave him a smile that made his insides quiver. "Because you haven't taken your eyes off me all night. I came in for a quiet pint, and what did I find? My sexy guy. Like it was fate or something. The name's Tony, by the way. And you're Harry. I caught that just now."

Harry swallowed. "But… why me? I mean, for God's sake, you're six-foot-tall of rugby player gorgeousness. I'm overweight and I work in a recruitment office. I'm… nothing."

Tony's eyes widened. "Not from where I'm standing, mate." He leaned in close. "I bet you've got a hairy chest, haven't ya?" He grinned. "Love me a guy with hair. And you're not overweight. You're just right—for me, that is."

Harry groaned. "Don't be so bloody stupid. I mean, *look* at me. I'm just a fat, ugly bloke. If you'd asked me on a date five years ago? Then yeah, I'd have considered it, but not now. Not when I look like this. I—"

Tony stopped him with a finger to Harry's lips, before leaning in even closer. "You don't tell me how I see you, all right?" His voice dropped to a barely audible, throaty whisper. "And if I want to invite you out for a drink, I'll fucking invite you out, you got that?" Before Harry could stop him, Tony slid his arms around Harry to give him a hug— before reaching down to squeeze his behind. Tony leered and whispered into Harry's ear, "Nice arse." Then he let go and sauntered out of the bar, without once looking back.

Harry stared after him, his heartbeat racing. *What the hell?* Then it crossed his mind what Tony's real intent had been, and he hurriedly searched his back pocket, to check his wallet was still there.

It was—along with a slip of paper, a phone number written on it.

What. The. Fuck?

Things like that just didn't happen. Not to Harry, at least. He stared at the scrawled number, as if that would somehow make the situation more real.

Nope. He still wasn't buying it. Gorgeous, sexy blokes did not just walk up to you and slip their phone number in your pocket. Unless…

For the first time, it occurred to Harry that this was someone's idea of a joke.

He stuffed the paper into his back pocket, grabbed three of the glasses and carried them carefully over to their table. Deb was grinning at him, and that only served to deepen his suspicion. He put down the glasses, ignoring her, and went to retrieve the rest. When he finally retook his seat, Deb leaned in.

"So, who was the sexy guy squeezing your arse?"

Like you don't know. Harry met her grin with a cool glance. "You didn't recognize him?"

Deb frowned. "Should I?"

It was a good act, but Harry wasn't convinced. "Oh, come on. The guy from the building site. The one who whistled." He gave her a hard stare. *Go on. Deny it.*

For a moment she stared back at him blankly, then her jaw dropped. "Well, fuck me. There *I* was, thinking my luck was in, an' he was after you the whole time?"

"You put him up to it, didn't you? The whistling? Turning up here when I just happened to be here?" Harry wasn't going to let her off the hook until she told him the truth. Although that blank stare was pretty convincing.

Deb widened her eyes. "God, no. As if I'd do that." She cocked her head to one side. "You pulled, didn't you, you dark horse?" That familiar grin returned.

Harry was momentarily shaken. If Deb hadn't had a hand in this, then either someone else had—who, he had no idea—or else….

He couldn't think like that. It would only get his hopes up, and then they'd get smashed to pieces when the truth finally came out. Because no way was such a gorgeous guy interested in him.

Ron tapped him on the knee. "Hey. Come on,

boss. We need you focused if we're going to get anywhere tonight." His eyes lit up. "You never know. Maybe our luck will change, and we'll be able to answer the questions."

Harry gave him a half-hearted smile in return, then took a long drink from his pint, almost spilling it when Deb dug her elbow into his ribs. "Hey, you never know. Maybe *your* luck has already changed."

No. No. No. Harry was not going to think about it. Even if Tony's number *was* burning a hole in his pocket….

Saturday went by in a blur. Harry cleaned the kitchen. Dusted the mantelpiece where he'd placed the slip of paper with Tony's number. Hoovered the living room. Dusted the mantelpiece. Cleaned the bathroom. Dusted the mantelpiece. Hoovered every carpet in the house. Dusted the mantelpiece at least fourteen more times.

That was when he picked up the paper, crumpled it into a little ball and dropped it in the waste paper basket, only to retrieve it five minutes later when he couldn't stop thinking about it. He reasoned that if he really wanted it gone, he would have set fire to it, not that the number wasn't already burned into his memory.

Harry changed the bed linen, bundling up the dirty shirts for the laundry. He caught sight of himself in the wardrobe door mirror and paused. "Why me?" he quietly asked his reflection. "What the hell does he see in me?" All Harry saw was a guy who had more around his middle than he needed. Okay, so his belly wasn't hanging in folds down over his belt, but it definitely wasn't the lean torso of his earlier years. Now it pushed gently against his top. And it wasn't as if he was flabby: that belly was still pretty firm—there was just too much of it, that was all.

He thought guiltily about the various gym memberships he'd taken out in the past few years— usually after New Year—only to cancel them by the end of February. Going to the gym was way too much effort. Harry wondered if he'd think differently if there was someone to impress. His thoughts went instantly to that damned slip of paper.

It had to be someone's idea of a joke.

It had to be a set-up.

Had to be. Because the alternative was… unthinkable. Unimaginable.

Unattainable.

Harry shoved aside such thoughts and dragged himself back into reality, which meant doing the laundry, then Strictly.

Sometimes reality just… sucked.

Chapter Three

Tony stirred, aware that his bedroom window was open, and a soft breeze was wafting into his room. He was unsure what had awakened him, until his nostrils caught the unmistakable aroma of freshly brewed tea. A mug stood on his bedside table, steam rising gently from it.

Aw, Mum. There were some compensations for living with your family. Some. Not many, not when you were Tony's age.

"Thanks, Mum," he shouted out, sitting up in bed and reaching for the mug.

"You're welcome," she yelled upstairs. "I'm off to work soon. You can come have breakfast once the morning rush has died down. TANYA! Get up! You've got ten minutes before I'm out of here. After that, you can get to work on the bus."

Tony smiled to himself. His sister wasn't the easiest person to rouse in the morning. He caught mumbling from the room next to his, and shortly after that, Tanya appeared in his doorway, still in her pink PJs, rubbing her eyes, her hair tousled.

"Thank God I don't have to put up with this much longer," she groused, before stumbling toward the bathroom.

"And Tony? Clean up the place before you come for breakfast, all right?"

"Yes, Mum."

"I'm about to put a load in the washing

machine. You got anything to add to it?" Footsteps on the stairs signalled her approach.

Tony stiffened. "No, that's okay. I'll do my own when your load has finished."

Mum leaned against the doorjamb. "Are you *still* going on about that? It was just the once, for goodness' sake."

Tony frowned. "Once was enough, when my Calvin Klein white briefs end up pink."

Mum pursed her lips. "Brief. That sums them up perfectly. What's wrong with boxers? I swear, you possess some of the skimpiest underwear I have ever seen. And what *is* the point of those jockstraps you're so fond of? All they do is leave your—"

"I thought you were getting ready for work?" he interjected. "Tanya's still in the bathroom." He knew it was low, using his sister to deflect his mum, but Christ, if she was going to start talking about his underwear again....

Mum rolled her eyes. "Qué lata, esa chica! Heaven knows how she's going to fend for herself when I'm not around to get her in gear."

Tony grinned. "That'll be Rocco's job."

His response worked perfectly. Mum narrowed her gaze, huffed, and strode toward the bathroom.

Tony leaned back against his pillows, sipping his tea. Tanya had the right idea. He couldn't *wait* to move out. All he needed was enough money saved to make it happen, because rents were getting higher by the second. It seemed that every time he thought he could afford a place, there was another hike in prices.

He needed a break. A change in his fortune. For some reason, what came to mind was his sexy bear, who now had a name. Harry.

Tony smiled again. *Come on, Harry. Call me. Ball's in your court, mate.* His dick jerked at the image in his head. Harry, naked in his bed, ready for Tony to—

The sound of his mum hammering on the bathroom door and her strident voice were like a splash of ice-cold water on his cock.

God, get me out of here.

Tony glanced at the street below, then chided himself. It was too early for Harry to make his appearance. Not that Tony anticipated any change in Harry's reaction. *If he was interested, he would have called.* And Tony's phone had been devoid of any such calls or texts all weekend, no matter how many times he kept giving it longing glances.

This might prove to be more difficult than I thought. Still, it was only Monday, and a whole week lay ahead of him. Plenty of occasions to show Harry he meant what he'd said.

"So, Tony," Steve called out. "Get much shagging in this weekend?"

Tony widened his eyes in mock surprise. "Why'd you ask? Didn't your brother tell ya?" Laughter erupted from the crew, and Steve's mate Donal gave Tony the thumbs up. Tony was used to such banter. It wasn't as if his sexuality was a secret, and when his crew teased, he always gave back as good as he got. Mostly, he kept to himself. He wasn't one to brag about his conquests, unlike a lot of his work crew.

Then again, what conquests? His sex life had been pretty quiet of late, although he had hoped that would change. Tony couldn't resist pulling his phone from his back pocket and glancing at the screen. Yeah, he knew he'd have felt it vibrate if a call or text came through, but there was no harm in checking, right?

Ben nudged him. "What's up? You've been doin' that since we clocked on. You expectin' a call or something? An' how did your weekend go? You were off for a drink last I heard from ya."

"Weekend was pretty much as usual." Tony glanced toward the street again, as a bus trundled by. It was still too early for Harry. *God, I've got it bad.* He'd been watching Harry ever since the sexy guy had caught his attention one late spring morning. Tony had had no clue as to his sexuality, but that didn't stop him from hoping. He'd seen Harry cast a few glances in their direction every morning, and that had been enough for him to make a move. A workman whistling was nothing new, after all. He'd gotten some appreciative glances from a couple of women, so getting Harry on his own the previous Thursday had been a godsend. Following Harry and his colleagues, to find them going to one of Tony's favourite pubs, had been nothing short of miraculous. Tony couldn't believe his luck. And after all the glances he had gotten?

Yeah, Harry liked men, thank God. But apparently not him, judging by his silent phone.

"Did you get stood up or something?" Ben asked quietly. "Because you're usually one of the most talkative bastards I know." His eyes twinkled. "And I mean that in the nicest possible way."

Tony sighed. Ben was his best mate, but right then, Tony didn't feel like sharing. "I tried something. It didn't come off. Let's leave it at that."

Ben gaped. "What? He didn't succumb to your charms?" He nudged Tony again. "You're getting' old, mate. Once you hit thirty, it's all downhill."

Tony wasn't laughing, however.

Ben put down his hammer and faced Tony. "Okay, who is it who's got your knickers in a twist?"

"I'll give you three guesses. Not that you'll need that many."

Ben's eyes widened. "Mr Travel Mug? Mate, I had no idea you were *that* interested in him. Oh… is… er…"

Tony gazed at him in mild surprise. "Not like you to be tongue-tied. Spit it out."

"That's how you like em?" Ben folded his arms across his broad chest. "So what's he then? I mean, since you've started enrichin' my vocab…" He counted off on his fingers. "I know twink, muscle Mary, sugar daddy…. He doesn't look like he's any of those."

Tony snorted. "He's not. He would come under the category of bear."

Ben blinked. "Bear?"

Tony nodded. "Bears are big, hairy guys. Then you've got your otters, who are slim and hairy, polar bears who are—"

"Stop right there!" Ben cackled. "I don't have my notebook on me to write all this down." He expelled a breath. "Wow. I never knew you could have so many different words to describe a guy."

Tony snorted again. "At least we have variety to describe gay guys. What have *you* got? As far as I can see, you're limited to big/small tits, big/small arse…"

One of the workmen called out, "You talking about Ben's sisters again?"

Tony laughed, and Ben waved off the remark, before returning his attention to Tony. "That's all there is, isn't there?" Tony picked up his saw and carried on preparing the length of wood, until Ben tapped him on the shoulder. "So, is that it then? Are you gonna leave it there?" When Tony gave him a quizzical glance, Ben rolled his eyes. "Mate. Stay on the subject. Mr. Travel Mug. Are you gonna just leave it there?"

"To be honest? I don't know. Hey, wanna play some darts after work?"

Ben scowled. "Don't change the subject. And if you're gonna make another move, think fast, because isn't this the time he usually walks past?" Ben's eyes gleamed. "Go on. Don't give up now. That's not the Tony *I* know."

"Looking a bit close there, Ben," Steve called out. "Something goin' on between you two that you wanna share?"

"Sure. We're engaged. Now fuck off," Ben said with a grin.

Steve snickered. "Yeah, right. I saw that last bird you went out with. You don't do dicks."

Ben's eyes gleamed. "Nah, I just work with 'em." Explosive laughter followed, and Tony smiled to hear it. He loved his job.

Then he recalled Ben's words. Maybe Harry needed to know Tony wasn't about to give up.

DENIM

By the time he got off the bus, Harry was in a foul mood. Stepping in dog shit on his way to the bus stop hadn't helped, especially when he kept getting looks from his fellow passengers, despite his best efforts to wipe off most of it on the grass. Wrinkled noses and pointed stares only served to piss him off even further.

Added to that, the bus was late, which meant there'd be a bunch of people lining up to get into the building, equally grumpy at having to stand around, waiting for him. Unless by some miracle, Sally had her keys on her, but that was too much to hope for.

The icing on the cake was the school-age kids sitting across from him. As soon as he'd taken a seat, the whispering had started, and Harry swore he heard them calling him names under their breath. He'd stiffened at the words, 'big fat gay bloke', and had done his best not to react. Except that had got him thinking for the rest of the journey. Did he look gay? What gave it away? And having his size rubbed in his face just added more shit to what promised to be a really shitty day. Because being late for work, when it wasn't any fault of his?

Harry hated that.

He got off the bus, ignoring the giggles that increased in volume as he did so, deliberately not glancing in their direction. Harry strode along the street, eyes front, determined not to look over at the building site, because the last thing he needed right then was to see Tony standing on that platform again, grinning at him.

Tony was standing by the fence, grinning at him, his fingers hooked through the wire. "Good morning. You're later than usual."

By then, Harry was in no mood to play nice. "Come on. You had your fun on Friday night. I figured it out, okay? Did you all have a laugh this morning? Did you tell them all about the fat guy?"

Tony's grin faded. "I don't recall giving my phone number to a fat guy. I gave my number to one of the sexiest guys I've ever seen."

Harry had had about as much bullshit as he could take. "Oh, just… fuck off." He left Tony and headed for the office, not looking back once.

This isn't remotely funny. And if he ever found out who was behind it, he'd make sure they knew it.

Chapter Four

By Wednesday morning, Tony's persistence had grown irritating. If it was indeed someone's idea of a joke, it had long since lost any semblance of being humorous. Harry had resorted to one syllable replies every time Tony said good morning to him as he passed the site, but Tony never seemed to take offence. Instead, he merely smiled.

Talk about not taking a hint, not to mention coming out with all that crap about Harry being a sexy bear. And then there were all the grins and chuckles at work Monday morning. Word had spread, like he'd known it would, and he'd lost count of the number of times he looked up from his desk to find someone watching him, smiling.

What amazed him was that his staff didn't see it for the joke it was. *They* all wanted to know if he and Tony were going to go out on a date.

A date? Are they fucking serious?

When it came time to leave the office Wednesday evening, Harry hung back while everyone left. It was already past six o'clock when he locked up the office, way later than his usual finishing time, but at least all the workmen had gone.

That uncomfortable feeling in his middle eased off a little.

The following morning, Tony was there, leaning on the scaffolding, watching Harry's progress along the street. No whistle this time, but

Harry was conscious of Tony's eyes locked on him, and it was a relief when he got inside the office. When evening came, he repeated the previous night's performance, relieved that once more the site was deserted. It wasn't that he was scared by Tony's behaviour, but all that attention made him feel uncomfortable.

Friday morning, he steeled himself to walk past the site, but there was no Tony. What surprised Harry was that instead of the relief he'd expected to feel, what assailed him was… disappointment.

Maybe he's changed sites. Maybe he's finally given up.

There was that wave of disappointment again.

Harry spent the rest of the day distracted. There were moments when for no explicable reason, Tony came to mind, and Harry couldn't help wondering why he hadn't shown up. Then he'd give himself a mental kick up the backside.

He was annoying. And don't say you believed that bullshit he fed you about finding you sexy. That inner voice was as practical as ever, but for the first time since Tony had accosted him with a piercing whistle, Harry made a discovery.

It had felt good that someone had liked him enough to show interest.

* * *

"Got anything planned for this weekend, Harry?" Deb asked as she grabbed her handbag from the back of her chair. Her eyes gleamed. "Got a wild party to go to?"

He snorted. "Sure. Thought I might find an orgy too while I'm at it." When she gaped at him open-mouthed, Harry burst out laughing. "Oh, sorry, I thought we were playing a game. You know, like, 'Make up something stupid that you'd never do in a million years', *that* kind of game." He rolled his eyes. "Because let's face it, me going to a wild party is about as likely as me going to an orgy."

Deb bit her lip. "Whatever you choose to do in your own time is no one's business but yours. And at least if you were at an orgy, you'd be gettin' some, which is a fat lot more than *I* am at the moment."

"I take it the fuck-me heels didn't work last week?" Ron asked with a grin.

"Chance'd be a fine thing," she replied gloomily, before nodding her head in Harry's direction. "Besides, *he* got the best lookin' bloke in there."

"I didn't *get* him," Harry protested.

"Only 'cause you turned him down," Brian called out from across the office. "I thought your luck was in there."

Harry cleared his throat. "When you've all finished trying to organise my love life, can I remind you that we've got a new guy starting Monday? Head office have finally sent us a replacement for Lou. His name's Simon Tanner."

Deb's eyes twinkled. "Ooh. Maybe my luck has changed after all." She winked at the others. "I could do with a little torrid office romance."

Harry laughed. "Poor Simon. He won't know what's hit him."

He waited until everyone had left the

building before stuffing his cup into his bag and doing a last check around. Then he locked the door and began his trek to the bus stop. The site was quiet, not really surprising seeing as it was POETS. Harry recalled the first time he'd used the acronym in a conversation with his mum, and the memory brought a smile. When she'd inquired what that meant, and he'd replied, 'Piss Off Early, Tomorrow's Saturday', she'd covered her mouth to smother the giggles.

The memory brought mixed emotions to the surface. There wasn't a day went by when he didn't think about her.

"And what have you been doing?"

Harry came to a dead stop at the sound of Tony's voice. Tony was leaning against the fence, hands stuffed into the pockets of his jeans—which only served to bring Harry's gaze to his crotch.

He struggled to look Tony in the eye. "Stupid question. I've been at work." Inside, Harry was soaring. *He hasn't left. He came back.*

There was something in Tony's knowing glance that told Harry he'd been rumbled. "Yeah, right. More like, you've been waiting for everyone else to leave, because you thought I'd have left by now. Well, too bad. I was waiting for you."

"What for?" Harry was past avoiding him by this point.

Tony straightened and met Harry's gaze head-on. "Come for a drink with me. One drink." He held up his hands. "That's all."

Harry was about to refuse, to make some excuse, when the thought occurred to him. *Why the fuck not?* It had been years since a good-looking guy had invited him for a drink, and seeing as this one showed no signs of giving up anytime soon…

"One drink," Harry confirmed. The way Tony's eyes lit up made him feel about ten feet tall. "Now?"

Tony grinned. "Too right, now. I'm not letting you out of my sight—you'll only change your mind."

"Do you have somewhere in mind?"

Tony's eyes sparkled. "Ever been to the Builders Arms?"

Harry shook his head. The name conjured up images of sawdust on the floor, a rough-and-ready clientele, a loud, raucous atmosphere… Not really his kind of place. Besides, these days he rarely ventured out of South Croydon.

Tony peered into the street and stuck out his hand to hail a passing taxi. "Trust me, you'll love it."

Harry had his doubts about that, but it was too late to back out now.

One drink. It's just one drink, remember?

Tony was enjoying himself. His choice of pub had been deliberate, and the look on Harry's face when he saw the hanging baskets overflowing with colourful blooms, the troughs of flowers above the door, and the wooden trough filled with climbing roses against a background of trellis, was worth it.

Harry gazed at him incredulously. "This looks… really nice."

Tony laughed. "Well, don't sound so surprised. I wasn't going to bring you to some dive, not on our first date." Before Harry could argue with his choice of words, Tony tugged his arm, guiding him through the main door. He knew from experience that the beer garden at the rear would be packed: it was a lovely summer's evening.

Inside, the pub was busy as usual, the air filled with the aroma of burgers and chips, and other such enticing smells. When a couple got up from the small, round table set in the bay window, Tony made a dive for it, pulling Harry along with him. He almost pushed him into one of the two high-backed red leather chairs in front of the window. "Now, what do you want to drink?"

Harry shrugged. "A pint of London Pride, thanks." He sniffed the air. "God, something smells good."

Tony simply smiled and strode toward the bar. *What do they say about the way to a man's heart?* In which case, a char-grilled burger and fries was guaranteed to have Harry's heart melting.

Harry couldn't get over how nice the pub was. The interior was filled with the warm hue of wood, from the floor to the tables and chairs, and the cladding around the bar and walls. The food was amazing: one taste of the burger had made him groan with pleasure, then he'd shut up quickly when Tony chuckled.

One pint had become two, then two had become three. Harry told himself he wasn't about to get drunk, not when he'd eaten, but it had been a while since he'd drunk anything more than a couple of cans of lager. The beer gave him a pleasant buzz, adding to the inviting atmosphere.

It came as something of a shock to realize he was enjoying himself.

Tony noticed, of course. He hadn't stopped grinning all night.

Harry could be gracious in defeat. "Okay, I might have had the wrong impression when you mentioned the name of this place."

Tony snickered. "No shit, Sherlock. That was kind of the idea." He looked around. "I do like coming here. It's got a good feel to it, especially when there's a match on. Plus, they have a quiz every week."

Harry frowned. "And yet you came to the Red Lion last week. Why?"

"Because of you," Tony said simply. When Harry blinked at him, he nodded. "I'd seen you all going there once before. That was before I really… noticed you. So, when you traipsed toward the pub, I figured I'd follow."

"Then it wasn't a coincidence?" He wasn't sure if he felt flattered or alarmed. "Don't you think that's a bit… stalker-ish?"

Tony gave a resigned shrug. "It was all I could think of at the time. The whistles had had no effect, that was for sure."

Harry's face tightened. "It was all a bit much, you know. The whistles, the stares…"

Tony stilled. "Did I make you uncomfortable?"

"Frankly, yes." When Tony's face fell, Harry sighed. "What did you expect? Some strange bloke comes up to me in the pub, compliments me on my arse, and leaves his number in my back pocket? And now I find out that you *followed* me there?"

"I had to find some way to get to talk to you." Tony's lips twitched. "Especially as my previous approach had been about as effective as a one-armed trapeze artist."

Harry smirked, then straightened his features. "You wouldn't have been joking if I'd reported you to the site management for harassment, would you?"

"Fuck." Tony sagged into his chair. "I never meant for you to feel uncomfortable. I had no idea if you even liked blokes. Then when I saw you up close in the pub, and you kept glancing over at me, I knew for sure." He peered at Harry. "Would you really have? Reported me, I mean."

Harry shook his head. He wasn't that kind of guy. "I'm just trying to get you to see that maybe the more direct approach would have been better." Taking note of Tony's gloomy expression, he patted his hand where it lay on the table. "Doesn't matter. We're here now, right?"

Tony's eyes shone. "That moment when I knew you liked guys? Best feeling ever."

"And now that we've chatted? Any regrets?" Harry held his breath. He couldn't deny Tony's pursuit of him was a stroke to his ego, but now that they'd finally connected…

Tony regarded him steadily, then reached over and squeezed his knee. "None whatsoever." Then he inclined his head toward Harry's empty glass. "How about another pint?"

Harry narrowed his gaze. "You're trying to get me drunk."

"What—so I can have my wicked way with you?" Tony gave an evil cackle and twirled an invisible moustache, before bursting out laughing. "You're safe with me, Harry. I'm a gentleman, promise." He got up and sauntered over to the bar.

Harry studied him, noting the firm arse encased in those gloriously tight jeans.

"Oh good, I'm safe," he muttered.

He wasn't sure if he was relieved or disappointed.

Chapter Five

His head was pounding.

His tongue felt like it was made of suede.

His throat was like sandpaper.

Just how much did I drink last night?

Harry had no recollection of how he got home. He peered beneath the sheets. Nor did he remember getting undressed down to his boxers. That in itself was a little strange: usually he slept in the nude. Then again, he couldn't remember the last time he'd been that drunk.

He glanced at the clock beside the bed. It was only eight-thirty, not as late as he'd thought, but late enough considering he had his usual weekend list of chores to complete. They would have to wait, at least until the manic drummer in his head took a break.

Harry sat up and swung his legs out of the bed. The first order of the day was coffee, before he'd even consider taking a shower. He stumbled to his feet, pulled on his robe, and lurched out of the bedroom, heading for the staircase. Harry glanced anxiously at the hall carpet, relieved to see he apparently hadn't been drunk enough to throw up once he'd gotten home.

He shuffled along the hall into the compact kitchen, making a beeline for the kettle. While he waited for it to boil, he pulled on the cord to roll up the blind, blinking in the harsh sunlight—and almost having a heart attack when someone yawned very loudly behind him.

"Christ!" he yelled, spinning around and catching his hip on the square table in the centre of the room. "Ow!"

Tony winced. "Careful."

"What are you—" Harry blinked at the sight before him. Tony stood in the doorway, wearing only his jeans, but *holy fuck,* they were unfastened, revealing the fuzz at the base of his belly.

Tony caught his glance and peered down at his crotch. "Oops." He hastily zipped up his jeans and fastened the button, before giving Harry a sheepish grin. "Sorry about the impromptu show. I've only just woken up." The kettle beeped and shut itself off, and his eyes widened. "Ooh, lovely. Tea, please. Milk, no sugar."

Harry stared at him. "But… what are you doing here?"

Tony regarded him with a mildly surprised expression. "I brought you home last night. Don't you remember? You were kinda out of it. I was worried about you, so I stayed the night." He gestured toward the living room with a flick of his head. "Slept on the couch." Tony cleared his throat. "The kettle's boiled, Harry."

Rubbing his hip, Harry turned his attention back to the kettle, opening the cabinet above it to retrieve another mug. "What time did we leave the pub?"

Tony snorted. "At chucking out time. You were looking a little green around the gills, to be honest. I just wanted to get you home. I didn't leave your room until you were fast asleep."

He turned around slowly. "Did you… undress me?"

There was that grin again. "Yeah. I stopped

at the underwear. I thought that was a step too far."

"Well, thanks for that." It was bad enough that Tony had seen as much as he did. Harry didn't think he'd have been able to look him in the eye if he'd removed everything.

Tony's eyes gleamed. "Not that I wasn't tempted, you understand." Harry narrowed his gaze, and he bit his lip. "Oh, come on. Don't tell me you wouldn't have done the same thing in my position."

Harry couldn't help his reaction—his gaze flickered down to Tony's crotch, the worn denim pale where his obvious—

He coughed, turned back to the kettle, reclicked it to bring it back to boiling, then swiftly produced hot tea and coffee.

Tony laughed. "I was about to ask, what does a guy have to do to get a mug of tea around here?"

"Here." Harry handed him the mug. He peered into the bread bin, then sighed when he caught sight of the word Bread on his shopping list, pinned to the fridge door by a magnet. "Not sure what I can offer you in the way of breakfast," he began apologetically, "but I—"

"You know what's the best thing after a drinking session?" Tony gave him a broad smile that reached his eyes, the skin crinkling around them. "A fry-up, and I know the very place."

"I'm sure I've got some cereal somewhere," Harry protested, but his stomach grumbled in reaction to the idea of a cooked breakfast.

Tony merely arched his eyebrows. "Good. It'll keep for another day then. Grab a shower if you want one, get dressed, and we'll be off."

Why is it so difficult to say no to him?

Harry gave up trying. "Fine. Give me twenty

minutes." And without waiting for a response, he left his coffee mug on the table and exited the kitchen. As he stomped up the stairs, he had to admit that close up, Tony had a gorgeous body.

Then why the hell is he interested in me?
It was a mystery he had yet to unravel.

Harry followed Tony into the cheery, busy cafe, inhaling the delicious smells that filled the air. Tony pointed to an empty booth in the corner. They slid along the red vinyl-covered, padded seats, and Tony handed him a menu from the stand that also contained ketchup, mustard, salt, pepper, and several packets of sugar and sweeteners.

"I can recommend the Valverde Special, and if you're really hungry, there's the Valverde Supreme. Same as the Special, only you get two sausages instead of one, three rashers of bacon, three eggs, and free refills of tea or coffee."

The Supreme was tempting, but Harry couldn't help feeling he'd seem greedy if he went for it. Then Tony leaned over the table and said in a low voice, "The thing I love about the Supreme? I eat that, and I don't need to have lunch. It does me the whole day."

Harry could live with that.

A young woman in a checkered apron came over to them, notepad in hand. She gave Harry a smile. "What can I get you?"

He ordered the Supreme, plus a mug of coffee, and she wrote it down, before disappearing behind the counter without even glancing at Tony. Harry stared after her in surprise. "She didn't take your order."

Tony laughed. "She didn't need to. My mum already knows what I want for breakfast."

Harry sat very still. "You've brought me to the cafe where your mum works?"

"Not exactly." Tony smiled. "I've brought you to the cafe that my mum *owns*. And the waitress? That's my sister, Tanya."

Harry scanned the menu again. "Valverde. That's your family name?"

"Yup. And before you ask, it's Spanish."

Harry cocked his head to one side. "Tony Valverde? Tony? Okay, what's your full name?"

He sighed. "Antonio Francisco García-Valverde. And my mum only calls me Antonio when I'm in trouble." He rolled his eyes. "Apparently, when she was carrying me, she had a thing for—"

"Antonio Banderas," Harry finished, grinning. When Tony gave him a speculative glance, Harry gave a slight shrug. "Let's say I'm acquainted with his films and leave it at that."

Tony narrowed his gaze. "I have a feeling I'm missing something."

"And you're not the only one who doesn't use his full name."

"Oh?"

Harry hesitated for a moment. "My full name is… Harrison."

Tony started laughing. "Let me guess. Your mum has a thing for Harrison Ford."

A brief pang pierced his heart. "She did, yeah."

Just then, an older woman approached their

table, her dark hair streaked with grey, and tied back in a bun. She placed a large plate in front of Tony, along with a very large white cup that smelled divine.

"Gracias, Mamá."

She bent over and kissed his cheek. "Y quién es?" Her gaze flickered in Harry's direction.

"Es un amigo, Harry."

Tony's mum gave Harry a warm smile. "Pleased to meet you. Tanya will be bringing out your breakfast shortly." She ruffled Tony's short hair, and he squirmed.

"Mum, please."

His mum laughed and left them alone. Harry snickered, and Tony grabbed a fork and held out it menacingly. "Say nothing," he intoned slowly.

Harry peered at his plate. "What's she brought you?" His plate was full of golden-brown, long strips that set Harry's mouth-watering.

Tony picked one up with his fingers. "These are churros," he explained. "Think of a doughnut, then imagine dropping the dough in long ribbons into hot oil. Some people also roll them in sugar, but not me. You dip them in this." He gestured to the cup.

Harry leaned over and sniffed its contents. "Is that chocolate?"

"Very thick chocolate." Tony proffered the strip. "Want to try?"

Harry took it, then dipped it in the thick, viscous liquid. Carefully holding his other hand beneath it to prevent drops, he brought the strip to his lips.

Oh my *God*. "That is amazing," he said with a groan once he'd taken a bite. "Do you eat like that all the time?"

Tony laughed heartily. "Hell no. If I did that, I'd soon be headed into Cardiac City. But when I come here for breakfast, Mum makes them for me."

Harry finished the delectable treat, then wiped his lips with a paper napkin. "Those are seriously addictive."

Tanya appeared, carrying a large oval plate, and a rack of toast. "I'll go and fetch your drinks," she said, disappearing once again.

Harry gaped at the plate. "I'll never eat all this." Food covered every inch of the white porcelain.

Tony patted his hand. "Don't worry. If you get stuck, I'll help." He rubbed his belly.

Harry couldn't help smiling. There was something about the laidback atmosphere in the bright, cheerful cafe that he found relaxing.

Tanya brought over two mugs and set them down. She gave a glance toward the counter, then slid into the booth beside Tony. "Are you still helping out tomorrow?" she asked urgently in a low voice.

"What's up?" Tony studied her closely. "Is Mum giving you hassle agai—"

She shook her head vehemently. "No, nothing like that. But some of my friends who were going to help us have pulled out." Tanya gave Harry an apologetic glance. "Sorry for interrupting your breakfast."

Harry decided he liked Tanya. "No problem. What's happening tomorrow?"

Before Tanya could reply, Tony said, "She's moving out to live with her boyfriend." He dropped his voice to a whisper. "Mum doesn't like it when we talk about Rocco. He's Italian." He peered at the table. "You've forgotten the milk, sis."

Tanya rolled her eyes. "Just add that to the list of things I've done wrong this morning. Mum is already on the warpath." She scooted off the seat and headed to the rear of the cafe.

"Why does it matter if her boyfriend is Italian?" Harry inquired quietly, watching in case his mum returned suddenly.

Tony did an eye roll that was so similar to Tanya's, it was uncanny. "Mum hates Italians, that's why. You'd think to hear her, that Tanya fell in love with him on purpose. Anyway, Rocco has found them a flat, and tomorrow she moves out."

Tanya returned with a metal jug full of milk. "Here you go."

Tony grabbed her arm. "I'll be there tomorrow, don't worry. And I'll bring an extra pair of hands." He stared across the table at Harry, a sudden grin flashing across his face. "You're coming too."

Before Harry could respond, Tanya opened her eyes wide. "Really? Oh, that's great. Thank you, so much." She beamed at him, before kissing her brother's cheek. "You're the best."

"Tanya!"

"Oops." Tanya flushed. "Back to work. Thanks, you two." She gave Harry a warm smile. "I didn't get your name."

"Harry."

She gave him a shy smile. "See you tomorrow, Harry." Then she was gone.

Harry picked up his fork and sliced the end of a sausage, saying nothing. He didn't have long to wait.

"Sorry for volunteering you like that, but it seems like she needs all the help she can get. If you've got stuff to do on Sunday, I'll make excuses for you. I should've asked before I opened my big mouth."

Harry curtailed Tony's apologies. "Tony? Shut up and eat your churros. It's fine. Trust me, I don't have anything planned that won't keep." Tony didn't need to know about his shopping and housework. Besides, it might even prove an interesting distraction. Because if it was a choice between doing the hoovering or spending time with Tony?

Harry knew which activity he preferred.

K.C. WELLS

Chapter Six

Tony peered along St. Peter's Road, but there was no sign of Harry. He pulled out his phone to check the time again.

"He'll be here," Tanya said, her arms full of a large cardboard box. "And in the meantime, we *do* have a van to unload, remember?" She grinned at him. Rocco appeared behind her, carrying a tall lamp.

"Sorry." Tony peered into the back of the van, pulled four boxes toward him, piled them up, then carefully lifted them.

"Lazy man's load, mate," Rocco called out. "You'll do yer back in like that."

"And how will you be able to work then?" Tanya added. "Not to mention, Mum'll kill me if you hurt yourself."

That much was true. Tony lowered his pile of boxes and picked up the top two. "I'm only thankful you're on the ground floor," he muttered as he followed them up the front steps into the building. Their flat was the only one on that floor.

Tanya snickered. "Yeah, I said the same thing when Rocco first brought me here."

"I still think you're crazy going for a flat with only one bedroom. What happens when you two fall out?"

"Hey. Nice positive thinking, mate," Rocco exclaimed. "Who says we're gonna fall out?"

Tony guffawed. "You haven't lived with my

sister yet." He put down the boxes on the living room floor, then yelped when Tanya smacked him across his backside. "Ow!"

"Serves you right. And in answer to your question, *he'll* be sleeping on the sofa."

Tony glanced across at Rocco, who was staring at her. Tony shrugged. "I tried to tell ya." He left them to go back outside to the van, arriving just as Harry came into view. "Hey, you found it."

Harry regarded him in mild surprise. "This place is only half an hour or so on the bus from mine." He glanced at the house. "This looks nice. Great neighbourhood too, from what I've seen so far."

Tony laughed. "The best part? It's miles from my mum's." Rocco appeared at the door, and Tony beckoned him over. "Rocco, meet Harry. I sort of strong-armed him into helping today."

Rocco laughed. He strolled over and held out his hand. "Nice to meet you, Harry. And yeah, I believe the part about strong-arming. It runs in the family."

"I heard that!" Tanya yelled from inside.

Harry burst out laughing, and Tony realized it was the first time he'd done that since they'd met. It was a great laugh too.

"Okay, what do you want me to do?" Harry asked.

Rocco pointed to the van. "Pick up something, take it inside, then rinse and repeat until we've emptied it. My stuff's already in the flat, and amazingly, we managed to cram all of Tanya's things into one van load."

Tony took a sharp intake of breath. "You're dicing with death, mate. Just saying. Because if you haven't worked it out yet, my sister has ears like a shithouse rat. She misses nothing."

Rocco snorted, grabbed two bags stuffed with clothes, and headed back to the house.

Harry watched him go. "He's a good-looking guy, isn't he?"

Tony shrugged. "I s'pose." He leaned in close and whispered, "He's not really my type. His arse is way too skinny, and he waxes his chest. Oh, and he's straight." He trailed his hand appreciatively down Harry's back, stopping before he reached his jeans. "Now this is more like it."

Harry narrowed his gaze. "Behave. That's your sister in there."

Tony guffawed. "Who wouldn't be in the least bit surprised to see me give your arse a quick squeeze." He removed his hand. "I'll behave though. Like I said, I'm a gentleman."

He wasn't sure how long he could keep up the act. Because right then? All he wanted to do was kiss Harry, and hope to God he returned the kiss.

"Tea's up!" Tanya carried a tray into the living room, where Tony, Harry and Rocco were sprawled on the three-seater sofa. Boxes filled every available space, and Harry didn't envy the job Tanya and Rocco faced to get the place sorted. His back bedroom at home was full of his mum's stuff, not to mention the floor-to-ceiling wardrobes in the tiny front bedroom, and the loft.

That's why I'm never moving. It'd take me

forever just to go through everything. And he wasn't sure he could bear to part with some of it. Too many memories.

"Is that the lot?" Rocco asked Tony, who'd been the last to come indoors.

Tony nodded. "One empty van. It didn't take us that long, did it?"

"Hola. Soy yo. Where are you all?"

Tanya gaped at Tony. "What's Mum doing here?" she hissed, before staring toward the door with a panicked expression. "*And* you left the door open." She hastily straightened her features as their mum entered the room, carrying a large box. "Mum? You didn't mention that you'd be coming today."

Her mum beamed. "Your aunt Marisa is minding the cafe. I thought I'd bring you all something." She handed the box to Tanya, who opened it and grinned, her previous annoyance vanishing.

"Okay. There's a packet of digestives in the kitchen for you lot," she told Tony, Harry and Rocco. "I'm keeping these."

Tony lurched up off the sofa and snatched the box from her hands. "Ooh, lemme see." He peered into the box and snickered. "Nah, these are far too good for you."

Their mum laughed and caught Harry's intrigued glance. "You'll have to forgive my children. They're like this every time I bake. It always has the same result." She gave them a pointed stare. "They forget their manners."

Tony was the first to react. He handed her the box with a sheepish expression that Harry found adorable. "Sorry, Mamá." He sat back down and gave Harry a gleeful smile. "She's made *tarta de*

Santiago. If you like almonds, you'll love it. And *torrijas*. They're like cinammon-flavoured pieces of fried bread. But best of all, there are *miguelitos*. They're fluffy, pastry pillows filled with chocolate cream." Tony licked his lips.

"Yeah, they're delicious," Tanya agreed, "but they also disintegrate into a million pieces as soon as you take a bite."

Rocco groaned. "They sound amazing."

Tanya's eyes danced with amusement. "Then *you'll* be doing the hoovering after we've finished eating them."

He shrugged. "I'm house-trained, me. I'm a dab hand with a hoover."

Harry couldn't help noticing how their mum blinked at that, before eyeing Rocco with approval. *I guess she might not be so hard on him after all.*

Tanya made coffee for her mum, then everyone sat to enjoy the pastries. Tony made room for her on the sofa, and sat on a huge beanbag instead that almost swallowed him whole, much to everyone's amusement. Their mum looked around the room, making comments to Tanya and Rocco, offering to bring them various items from home that might fit well in the flat. She chatted with Harry, asking him about his job, and how he'd met Tony. Harry had caught the glint in Tony's eye before he could open his mouth to respond, and made sure to give a version where Tony was *not* whistling lewdly from a scaffold. Somehow, he didn't think that would go down well with her. Judging by Tony's relieved expression, he'd done the right thing.

Harry hadn't felt this relaxed in a long while, but the cheerful atmosphere brought with it an unexpected sting. Tony's mum reminded him so much of his own mum, and just listening to her talk, seeing her laugh with her kids, brought home to him how much he missed her. When tears pricked the corners of his eyes, Harry wiped them away quickly, but not quick enough that Tony didn't see him. Thankfully, he said nothing, and Harry pushed aside his memories and joined in the conversation.

Eventually, their mum left, albeit reluctantly, and Harry was filled with warmth at the sight of her hugging Tanya. He recalled how his own mum had been, when Harry had left home to live in London. Anyone would have thought he'd been moving to the other side of the country. Harry guessed it was a huge thing when the chicks finally left the nest.

Of course, he hadn't stayed away all that long, had he?

After saying goodbye to Tanya and Rocco—and after promising to accept an invitation to dinner once the flat was sorted—Harry left them on their doorstep and walked with Tony to the end of the paved parking area in front of the building, bracketed by two huge trees. They turned left onto the road, both walking slowly, in no hurry.

"So, what's on the agenda for the rest of your Sunday?" Tony asked him.

Harry snickered. "There's not much left of it, is there? A bit of TV, maybe some ironing, so I'm ready for the week." Harry had to admit, it sounded deathly dull.

"Thanks again for helping out."

He smiled. "I was happy to. And it was a good day." He'd enjoyed himself, and it had been fun getting to know Tony's family a little better. Rocco seemed like a solid kind of bloke, and Tanya was clearly head over heels. *Must be nice to feel like that about someone.*

"It was," Tony agreed. Harry waited for him to make some comment about his brief emotional state, but to his relief Tony maintained his previous silence.

Harry came to a halt at the bus stop. "This is me," he said, reluctantly. He didn't want to leave.

Tony's eyes glittered. "Do I get a kiss goodnight?"

Harry laughed. "Well… seeing as you've been such a gentleman…."

Tony snorted. "If you only knew the effort *that* took." When Harry frowned, puzzled by the remark, Tony shifted a little closer. "I've wanted to kiss you since that night in the Red Lion." His voice took on a husky quality that made Harry's dick stiffen.

That sent Harry's heart thumping. "Then let me put you out of your misery," he said, his voice shaking a little.

Tony caught his breath, then leaned forward to press his lips lightly against Harry's.

God, that was… sweet. What Harry loved most was that Tony plainly didn't give a flying leap who saw them kiss.

Then two hands squeezed where Harry hadn't expected them. "Tony? Why are your hands on my arse?" Not that he was complaining.

Tony brushed his lips against Harry's ear. "Told ya. You've got a nice arse." He released Harry and took a step back when a bus trundled into view. "Now get that cute arse home, and I'll see you tomorrow morning." He was still grinning. "I'll be the one whistling."

"I look forward to that." Harry was seized by an urge to return Tony's kiss, but the bus had already stopped, its door open and the driver regarding them with amusement. He clambered on board, giving Tony one last wave as the door closed.

Harry stuffed his Oyster card back into his pocket and dropped into an empty seat.

It had gone from being a good day to a fantastic day, in the space of one kiss.

Chapter Seven

Harry swung his jacket over one shoulder, his bag over the other, and strolled along the street toward the recruitment office, humming to himself. It was a glorious early August morning, and the air was already warm. As he neared the building site, a thought struck him, making him smile. A warm day meant Tony would probably be working in only his tight jeans and boots again.

Heaven.

But as he came into view of the fence, he realized he wasn't the only one hoping to catch sight of a strapping workman wearing very little. A tall, slim guy in a tight-fitting, pale blue shirt, and red trousers that appeared almost sprayed on, was standing by the fence, his fingers curled through the wire, watching the men at work and grinning. He turned his head as Harry approached, his eyes hidden behind round, dark brown sunglasses.

"Just admiring the, er, workmanship," he said, his grin not diminishing in the slightest.

Harry said nothing. A glance to his left revealed Tony to be nowhere in sight, and that made his heart sink a little. He contented himself with the knowledge that Tony would probably be around that evening. Harry passed by the young man, picking up his pace, and headed for the office.

To his surprise, the younger man followed him. By the time Harry was unlocking the main door, the guy had caught up with him. Then the light dawned. "Would you be Simon Tanner?"

The young man removed his sunglasses. "Guilty as charged. I wanted to be here before anyone else arrived, but I got side-tracked by the… view." He waggled his eyebrows. "And would you be Harry Forrest?"

Harry regarded him mildly. "Perhaps 'Mr. Forrest' might have been more appropriate, don't you think?" Not that anyone in the office referred to him in that manner—they'd all worked with him for at least a couple of years—but he'd expected a slightly more formal greeting, considering Simon was meeting his new boss for the first time.

Not exactly an auspicious beginning.

Simon blinked, then stared at him as if he'd said something in a foreign language.

Harry sighed inwardly. Not auspicious at all.

It was almost time for lunch, Harry noted as he finished typing an email to head office. Judging by the chatter that had increased exponentially, he wasn't the only one who'd noticed. Generally, the office closed for an hour, a rule that Harry had instigated when he'd become manager. It was often a lively time, and he rarely saw anyone eating alone: his staff members were a gregarious bunch.

Harry had arranged for Ron to keep an eye on Simon, to show him the ropes. Having the boss watch you could be pretty intimidating, and after the way he and Simon started out, maybe having Ron as his mentor for a while would prove less problematic. Harry had caught a lot of laughter from the area where Simon's desk was located, so maybe he was settling in just fine.

He got up to go into the small kitchen. It contained a huge fridge, a small freezer, a microwave and a kettle, as well as the all-important coffee machine. Deb was in charge of that, and she ensured the pot was kept full. There wasn't really space to sit down, so everyone ate at their desks.

Harry poured himself a coffee, the plan being to get in there before everyone else had the same idea. Ron entered shortly after him, but then closed the door. "Can I have a word?"

Harry stilled. "Sure." The kitchen was one of only two private spaces in the entire office: the other was the bathroom. The office's large, open-plan look was great, but it didn't really allow for a quiet word when one was required.

Ron took a deep breath. "Okay, before I tell you what's on my mind, can I just check one thing? You wouldn't call me a homophobic sod, would you?"

Harry arched his eyebrows. "Not the first words that come to mind," he commented dryly. "Where on earth is this going?"

Ron held up his hands defensively. "I had to get that out into the open, before I go any further. It's important that you realize I'm not saying... what I'm about to say... because of prejudice, all right?" He gave the door a sidelong glance, as if he expected it to open at any second.

Harry didn't like this one bit. "Ron, please, whatever's on your mind, spit it out."

He let out another heavy sigh. "Okay, it's

that new guy, Simon. If he carries on like this, I'm gonna fucking kill the little toe-rag."

Harry smothered his gasp. "Whoa. What's he done to get you this riled? He's only been here—" Harry consulted his watch. "—four hours."

Ron's eyes widened. "I know! But it's the way he stands so close when he's talking to me. It's almost like he's about to rub himself up against me, like a cat in heat."

Harry's stare must have rivalled Ron's. "Seriously?"

Ron nodded. "He leans over my desk. He puts his hand on my shoulder. It's not like you can miss it. He's about as subtle as a brick through a plate glass window. And God, talk about innuendos. He's full of 'em. I mean, it must be bleedin' obvious that I'm not gay, not interested, not in a million years, but he doesn't seem to notice." He took a deep breath. "Can you have a word with him? Tell him this really isn't on."

Harry put down his mug. "Yes, I could," he said carefully, "but to be honest, it needs to come from you first. I'd step in if he persisted after that." He tilted his head to one side. "Have you told him to lay off?"

Ron lowered his gaze. "Not as such. I mean, I haven't encouraged him, you understand, but—"

"But you haven't actually come right out and told him where to get off," Harry confirmed. Ron shook his head. Harry came to a decision. "Okay. Here's what we do. You take him aside when everyone's in here, acting like a swarm of locusts while they try to grab their pasta salad, tofu or whatever it is they're eating today, and you have a quiet but firm word with him. Make sure he knows that the next time it happens, that quiet word will be with me, it *will* go on his record, and head office *will* get to hear about it."

Ron was breathing more easily. "Yeah, yeah. I can do that." He stared down at his body. "I keep wondering why on earth he'd be fixated on me. I mean, I'm not exactly God's gift, right?"

"Hey, don't put yourself down. You're a good-looking man. And right now, he's giving gay guys a bad name." Then he snickered. "What do the girls make of him?"

Ron groaned. "God, they think he's cute. They're already trying to arrange a Friday night out in Soho—something about G-A-Y?" His eyes widened. "When I came in here, Simon was talking to Brian. Poor sod. I'd better get back out there. I swear, no guy's safe around him. Well, except for you, of course." And with that, he yanked the door open and left the kitchen.

Harry was momentarily stunned by Ron's final throwaway remark. *Except for me because I'm the boss?* Or perhaps his words had another meaning—that Simon wouldn't be interested in him because of how he looked. He ran a hand over his all-too-solid belly, imagining how it must look to someone as slim and gorgeous as Simon. Because he *was* gorgeous, there were no two ways about it. Harry might not like him all that much, but he could be honest about why Simon might appeal to a lot of gay men.

I remember when I looked like that. But that had been a lifetime ago, and no gay guy in their right mind would look at him twice nowadays. A wave of bitterness and resentment swept over him.

The thought came to him like a gentle prod, a

quiet voice filtering through his head.

Tony looks at you though. Tony seems to like what he sees, doesn't he?

Harry opened the fridge and stared at the large plastic container of chicken and bacon pasta salad he'd bought from Tesco's on the way to the bus.

And maybe he'd like me even more if I stopped stuffing myself with food like that.

He closed the fridge and returned to his desk. He could do without lunch for one day.

Tony watched the steady stream of people walking past the site, all heading home or wherever it was they were going. Not that Tony cared—all that interested him was Harry. He hoped their weekend together had brought an end to Harry avoiding him.

Then he grinned when he caught sight of Harry, his jacket slung over his bag, walking slowly. Tony's grin died as he took in the weariness that seemed to surround Harry like an invisible cloak. Tony grabbed his jacket and bag, and hurried over toward him.

"Hey, you not intending to stop and say hi?" he asked as he drew nearer.

Harry came to a halt, giving him a smile that didn't reach his eyes. "Hi. Sorry. I was in a world of my own. Must have been, if I didn't see you."

Tony stilled. "Tough day?"

Harry gave a shrug. "Could've been better,

yeah. To be honest, I just want to go home and put my feet up."

"Sounds like a good plan." Tony took a step closer. "Except you're not going anywhere without one of these." He curved his hand around Harry's cheek and leaned in to kiss him. Nothing heavy, a chaste meeting of lips, but he lingered there, drinking in Harry's scent, his senses stirred by the smell of Harry's sweat, musky and powerful.

When he broke the kiss, Harry let out a quiet, happy sigh. "I needed that."

"Plenty more where that came from," Tony assured him. "Now get off home, relax, have a good night's sleep, and before you know it, you'll be waving good morning to me."

"I missed you this morning," Harry said in a rush.

It was the sweetest declaration Tony had heard yet. "Yeah, sorry about that. I had to pick up some supplies from the builders' merchants." He couldn't help himself. Tony moved closer and kissed Harry again, only this time he cupped his nape, pulling him in. Harry laid his hand on Tony's shoulder, seemingly lost in the embrace, until he cleared his throat and took a step back.

"What is it about you that makes me lose all sense of decorum?"

Tony snickered. "Overrated stuff, decorum." Feeling bold, he reached down and gave Harry's arse a light tap. "Home. I'll see you tomorrow. And keep Friday night free."

"Oh? Something happening Friday?" Harry's eyes sparkled with humour.

Tony's grin faded. "You and me, on a date. Not some drink in a pub—a real, honest-to-goodness date."

Harry's breathing hitched. "Okay," he said slowly.

Tony gave him a peck on the lips. "See? Life's much better when you just go with the flow."

"It'll go even better if you stop smacking my arse," Harry told him, narrowing his gaze.

Tony laughed. "Oh, now you're demanding the impossible. My hand clearly has an affinity for your delectable rear end."

Harry snickered. "Tomorrow, then." He gave Tony a smile that warmed his insides. "Thanks for waiting for me." Harry walked off, glancing over his shoulder at intervals, until he reached the corner and Tony lost sight of him.

If I get that response, I'll wait every single day.

Chapter Eight

It still amazed Tony that such a simple little thing like waving good morning to Harry could make him feel on top of the world. It felt like he was starting the day on the right note. He watched as Harry disappeared from view, then picked up a sheet of insulation and carried it over to the timber-framed walls, whistling.

"*Someone* got out of bed on the right side this morning," Ben commented. Tony glanced across to find him smirking. "An' whose bed was that?"

"My own, unfortunately." It was weird not having Tanya around. He knew Mum was happy that he was living at home, but for God's sake, he was *thirty.* He wanted a space to call his own, where he could live without the fear of his mum coming into his room to pick up laundry, and finding things he *really* didn't want her to lay eyes on.

Ben snorted. "You're slippin' up, mate. You're usually a fast worker." He waggled his eyebrows. "Is Mr. Travel Mug playing hard to get?"

Tony sighed. "Not exactly. I'm the one taking my time. I took him to the caff on Saturday."

Ben's eyes widened. "You took him to meet your mum? Blimey." He glanced at the others who were working a few feet away, then shifted a little closer to Tony. "Mate, that sounds... serious."

Tony put down the blade he'd been using to cut up the insulation board. "Not yet, but I'm working on it." He smiled. "We're going on a date Friday." He already knew exactly where he was taking Harry.

It was going to be an interesting night.

"Hey, Princess, your stalker's 'ere," Steve called out. He gestured with his thumb toward the street. He pursed his lips and blew Tony a kiss.

Ben looked to where Steve was pointing. "Now *he's* a twink, right?"

"Huh?" Tony straightened and peered into the street. "Him again?" It was the same guy he'd seen the previous three days. "Not interested."

A loud whistle ripped through the air. "Nice pecs, sexy!"

Tony crossed over to the scaffolding and gazed down at the slim guy with the perfectly styled hair and fashionable shades. "Aren't you gonna be late for school?" he yelled. The twink gave an exaggerated pout, and Tony rolled his eyes. Such a fucking baby. "Go on, get out of here. Your nappy needs changing." He went back to his task, still shaking his head. The guy was maybe younger than Tanya, but judging by the attitude, he probably believed he was God's Gift.

"Not your type?" Steve said in a loud voice.

"Not cooked long enough," Tony said with a grin. "I like 'em a little older. And on that note, say hi to your dad for me? Tell him same time, same place, next week." He leered, and raucous laughter erupted from his workmates. Tony went back to his task, whistling merrily, Harry on his mind.

The weekend couldn't arrive fast enough.

Harry stared at his reflection in dismay. When was the last time he'd bought a pair of jeans? His present pair were worn, and not in a fashionable way. He couldn't wear them. Okay, so they were all right for breakfast in the cafe, or helping Tanya and Rocco move stuff, but on a date? He needed to look smart, and they were worn to buggery.

Time to go shopping. At least it was only Wednesday. He could go into London straight after work the following evening. Maybe he could buy a new shirt while he was at it. An image of Simon rose in his mind, immaculately dressed, in a shirt so tight you could plainly see his naturally flat belly, reminiscent of the one Harry has possessed at that age.

He can probably stuff his face all day and still *be as slim as a rake. The bastard.*

Harry gazed at his belly.

Yeah, maybe he didn't need a shirt *that* tight.

He shucked off his jeans, then stepped into a pair of baggy sweatpants. Perfect for a night on the couch. He went downstairs and into the kitchen to decide what ready meal would be his dinner. The frozen meat lovers pizza was tempting, and he was ravenous. He'd skipped lunch again, the third time that week. Harry wondered how long he'd have to keep that up before he would notice a difference in his waist measurement. Expecting a change after three days was a bit much. Maybe if he skipped a couple of dinners too?

Sighing, he closed the freezer door. He didn't

really need pizza anyway.

The rumble his stomach gave out was almost as if it was arguing with him.

Harry pulled the curtain closed, stepped out of his black office trousers, and tried on the first of the three pairs of jeans he'd plucked from the rack. There had been a few different styles in size thirty-two waist, and he'd chosen a dark blue pair, a black pair and a fashionably faded pair.

The dark blue pair didn't seem to want to even *contemplate* closing. The black pair was no better. And the faded pair? Harry let out a groan of sheer frustration. He tugged at the waistband, trying his hardest to get it anywhere near to closing, and swearwords tumbled from his lips.

"Can I help at all?" The male voice had a Mediterranean lilt to it.

"No!" Harry blurted out.

"Are you sure? I'm just asking, because it doesn't sound like you're having a lot of success back there."

Harry sighed. "I'm… having a little difficulty getting into the jeans, that's all." That had to be the understatement of the year.

"What size did you take in there?"

"Thirty-two. That's the size I usually wear."

"Mm-hmm. They do tend to run a little on the smaller side. Let me find you another pair to try on." Footsteps moved away from the curtain, and Harry took a deep breath. A minute later, the curtain parted enough for a hand to thrust a folded pair of black jeans through the gap.

"Try these. They're a thirty-six."

Harry wanted to shout that *no way* was he that size, but he tried them on anyhow. The jeans fit perfectly, closing with ease.

Like that mattered. Harry was not about to buy a pair two sizes bigger. He couldn't be a thirty-six-inch waist. He *couldn't* be.

"Can you find me a size thirty-four?" he asked.

The curtain was flung back, and Harry came face-to-face with the shop assistant, whose name badge proclaimed him to be Arnold. He was roughly the same height as Harry, but with a black beard, neatly trimmed moustache, dark eyes, and a body Harry would have killed for.

Arnold narrowed his gaze. "Now look. You're a cute bear, and—"

"Excuse me?" Harry stared in astonishment.

Arnold merely rolled his eyes. "Oh, sweetheart. Come *on*. Thirty-six is baby bear size. You were trying on a thirty-two, so no wonder you were having problems. Your waist wouldn't fit into a size thirty-two, your legs neither." His wide smile revealed white, even teeth. "Trust me, okay?" He closed the curtain, leaving Harry still open-mouthed. Seconds later, Arnold was back, pulling it open again and handing Harry another pair of jeans. "Try these. They've got a tapered leg, so they'll flatter you, but your big, lovely thighs will fit into them, and so will your waist."

Harry arched his eyebrows. "Do you talk like this to all your customers?"

There was that wide grin again. "Only the

bears, sweetheart. You should see me when I'm on holiday in Sitges. Talk about bear heaven." When Harry frowned, Arnold nailed another eye-roll. "Sitges? Near Barcelona? Every September they have Bear Week, and I get to spend the entire holiday surrounded by gorgeous specimens." He let out an exaggerated sigh, then straightened his features. "And no, you don't need a thirty-four. If you tried sitting in a pair that size, it would be painful. And the only way on this earth that you'd get into a size thirty-two? We're talking *lots* of elastic, and we don't *do* a maternity version. Now try those on, and call me when you're in them." He pulled the curtain back briskly.

It wasn't until he'd zipped up the jeans that Harry realized Arnold actually liked the way he looked. There'd been no disgust, only obvious interest. And he had to admit, Arnold knew his stuff: the jeans looked pretty damn good.

"Ready?" Arnold called out.

Harry pulled back the curtain and stepped out onto the shop floor.

"Turn around, let me see."

Harry did a slow turn, and Arnold beamed at him. "Perfect. Okay, that's the jeans sorted. Hang them over the rail when you're done, and I'll take them to the cash desk for you. Now, is there anything else you'd like to try on? Because I have some tees that would be amazing on you."

T-shirts sounded like a step out of his comfort zone of baggy sweaters and office shirts, but he'd gone this far. "And a couple of casual shirts too." *Come on, I'm thirty-five, not sixty-five.*

Arnold's face was alight with enthusiasm. "Leave it to me. I'll bring you a selection." He hurried off toward the racks near the shop's entrance.

Harry had to smile at Arnold's eagerness and energy. He stepped back behind the curtain and removed the jeans, trying not to think about the change in size. *Tony doesn't need to know what size I am, right?* The fact that he'd let himself go so badly, made Harry's stomach clench.

Then he reasoned that if he kept up his newly acquired habit of skipping meals, before long he might need the size thirty-four pair after all. A good enough excuse to miss dinner. Again. It wasn't like he was contemplating *starving* himself, just cutting out a meal here or there.

Arnold appeared at his changing booth, holding out four or five shirts on hangers, and three or four folded tees. "Try these on. Whatever you don't want, just leave them here. I'll tidy up later." He flashed those perfect teeth again. "It's what they pay me for, after all." Arnold sauntered off, with only the tiniest swing to his slim hips.

Harry watched him with amusement. Arnold was a character.

It didn't take Harry long to pick out a black cotton shirt that suited him. Then he reasoned that there might be other dates after this one, and maybe it would be good to be prepared. He wasn't about to wear the same shirt twice. Harry unfolded the top T-shirt, to see a large bear paw print across the chest.

Arnold was definitely a character.

His items piled up on the cash desk, Harry stood as Arnold carefully folded each piece of clothing and placed it inside the large stiff paper bag. When he got to the pair of jeans, Harry gave an unhappy sigh, and Arnold glanced up sharply.

"They looked great on you."

Harry couldn't deny that. "It's just the size, that's all."

Arnold pursed his lips, reached under the desk, and pulled out a pair of scissors. He neatly snipped the size label from the jeans, and gave Harry a triumphant smile. "See? They're not a size thirty-six now. They're yours." He locked gazes with Harry, as though daring him to argue the point.

Harry knew when he was beaten. "Fine," he said resignedly.

Arnold beamed again. "There's a good bear." He tilted his head to one side, his eyes gleaming appreciatively. "Is there a possibility I might see you one year in Sitges?"

Harry coughed and hastily handed over his credit card. He had no clue how to answer that. Bear week?

Maybe it was time he did a little research.

Chapter Nine

Harry thought his heart had been in overdrive ever since he'd received Tony's text that morning.

East Croydon rail station, 7.00pm.

He'd dashed out as soon as the office had closed, past the empty building site, and hurled himself onto the first bus. Once home, he'd taken a shower that had to be a contender for the Guinness Book of Records—he was *not* going to be late. When the Uber pulled up outside his house, Harry was ready in his new jeans, black boots and black cotton shirt. No jacket required—the evening was far too warm for that.

That first sight of Tony leaning against the station wall, watching the world go by, had set off yet another surge of panic. It had been years since Harry had gone on a date, and back then, a night out generally meant one thing—fucking. What scared him was that he had no idea what to expect with Tony. Harry was no fool: he knew Tony was taking things slowly for his benefit.

Then he watched as Tony's eyes lit up, and the nerves that had plagued him slowly seeped away.

It was going to be okay.

"Don't *you* scrub up nice?" Tony looked him up and down, and Harry's heartbeat pounded. "Yeah, very nice. Looking good, Harry." He straightened, strolled over to where Harry stood, and kissed his cheek. Tony reached down and grabbed

Harry's behind with one hand. "And this arse makes a good pair of jeans look even better."

"Glad you approve." Harry silently sent a Thank You to Arnold. "Sorry about the beard." He'd sworn very loudly when his shaver had broken as he was getting ready. What made the situation worse was that he didn't have a single razor in the house.

Tony gaped. "You *are* kidding, right? You were gonna shave it off?" He rolled his eyes. "Now why would you want to go and do a stupid thing like that?" He reached up to caress Harry's beard. "This is perfect."

Harry ignored his increased heart rate. "So, want to tell me where we're going?"

Tony released him. "Train to Victoria first, then the tube."

When nothing else was forthcoming, Harry chuckled. "That's all I get?"

"Details to be released on a need-to-know basis, and right now, you don't need to know." Tony's eyes twinkled. "You're just gonna have to trust me."

Easy for him *to say.* Harry was having palpitations. "Look, it's been a while, okay? Since I did this, I mean."

Tony paused at the ticket barrier, regarded Harry keenly, then smiled. "Relax. You look amazing. And all we're doing is going for a meal, a drink, and maybe a club later. Nothing heavy. I just want you to enjoy yourself." He flushed. "And just so you know? I'm a bit nervous too. I've been thinking about this all week."

It was such a change from the usually confident, laidback Tony he'd come to know, that Harry stilled. "Really?"

Tony laughed. "Is it such a surprise to learn I'm human too?" He snorted. "God, I'm as insecure as the next man."

"Well, if the next man happens to be me, that's *really* insecure," Harry joked.

Tony jerked his head toward the platform. "So, are we catching this train or what?"

Harry laughed. "Lead the way."

"God, when was the last time I was on Old Compton Street?" Harry mused as they turned the corner. Not that it had changed much: there were more places shut down than he remembered previously, however.

Tony laughed. "I come here a lot less than I used to. And as for Pride, hell no. You couldn't shove a cigarette paper between two guys on this street, it's that packed. Every single club is full to bursting. Having said that, the atmosphere is fantastic."

Harry stared as they crossed the street. "Wow. I can't remember the last time I was in Balans."

"Ah, now that *has* changed," Tony said as they approached Balans' door. "It's less of a bar, more of a restaurant these days." He paused. "Ready to eat?"

"We're having dinner here?"

Tony held the door open for you. "After you."

The tables were already filling up, but

thankfully there was space at the rear. Harry preferred that: he hated being on show, and the back felt more private. Their waiter was a tall, skinny guy with a very prominent ginger beard. He handed them the large laminated menu cards, then almost danced away to another table.

"He's a character," Harry murmured.

Tony chuckled. "Being a character probably earns him more tips. Now, what are you drinking?"

Harry gave him a hard stare. "The last time you asked me that, we ended up very drunk."

Tony snickered. "Nah, that part comes later." He peered at the menu. "I'll just have a coke." When Harry blinked, he flashed him a grin. "Plenty of time for alcohol after we've eaten. And I know exactly what I want. A burger, with their huge onions rings, and chips."

That sounded delicious, even if it was way much more than Harry wanted on his plate. He perused the card. Somehow, he didn't think Tony would be content to let him order a green salad, so he went with the next best thing. "I'll have a coke too, and the chicken and bacon cobb salad, no dressing." Harry placed his menu on top of Tony's, then leaned against the padded back.

"You sure? A salad?"

"I had a big lunch," he lied.

Dinner was very pleasant. Tony told funny stories about his family and working on various building projects, and Harry couldn't remember a time when he'd laughed so much. Laughter seemed to have been a rare commodity in his life the last few years. His dad hadn't been a humorous man, and it hadn't been uncommon for Harry and his mum to share sideways glances when Dad failed yet again to see the funny side of something.

I'm getting old before my time. Maybe spending time with Tony would change that.

Harry ate about half his salad, claiming to be full. After a week of eating one or two meals a day, he hadn't noticed any great change in the mirror. He knew it would take time.

When the bill arrived, Tony got out his wallet, but Harry wasn't about to have that. "If you won't let me pay for dinner, then at least split the bill with me." Harry gave him a mock-glare. "Or we don't be doing this again."

Tony looked like he was going to argue, but then shrugged. "Fine." He pulled out a couple of bank notes and tossed them onto the table. "That should cover half." Then he put away his wallet and grinned. "But I get to buy your first drink."

Harry blinked. "Are you going to tell me *where* we're drinking?"

"Around the corner, in the Duke of Wellington. Do you know it?"

He shook his head. He recalled walking past it many a time when he was younger, but hadn't felt compelled to go inside. One look at the clientele had told him all he needed to know. "It wasn't really my kind of place."

"Wasn't?" Tony cocked his head to one side. "And how old were you at the time?"

Harry shrugged. "Twenty, twenty-one."

Tony gave a knowing nod. "Yeah, I can see why you wouldn't have been interested back then. *Now*, however? Whole different kettle of fish."

"What do you mean?"

Tony's eyes sparkled. "Wait and see."

They left Balans and walked side by side to

the end of the street, where Tony took a left, then pointed to a bar on the corner where men were congregating outside, smoking and drinking. A bouncer admitted them, and Tony led him into a packed interior, most of the guys standing. A staircase curved up in a spiral, and Tony pointed up.

"It'll be less busy upstairs."

Harry followed close behind Tony as they tried to get to the bar, through a crowd of guys who were giving them appreciative glances. Tony raised his voice to be heard above the music, and ordered them a couple of beers. It wasn't until Harry was gazing around them at the bar's patrons that two things fully sank in.

One—most of the men were about the same age as Harry, maybe older, and all of them were solidly built guys, a lot of them with beards or tattoos, or both.

Two—they were looking at him.

The man nearest to him looked Harry up and down, and muttered, "Fuckin' 'ell." He dug the guy next to him in the ribs with his elbow. The guy gave Harry a warm smile.

"Can we get you a drink?"

Harry returned the smile, albeit at a slightly dimmer wattage. "Thanks, but I'm sorted."

"Well, we'll be here when you're ready for another," he said as Tony handed Harry a pint. The guy didn't even give Tony a glance, but leaned in closer to whisper in Harry's ear, "And we'd be ready for whatever you felt like doing." Then he straightened and winked at him.

Tony nudged him. "Upstairs?" His lips twitched.

Harry nodded, and they picked their way

through the crowd to climb the narrow, winding stairs. The upper space proved to be very different, with red-and-black carpet, tables and chairs, and even a small, comfortable-looking couch. Tony inclined his head to the far corner, and Harry followed him to an empty table, behind which a red leather-covered couch stood against the wall.

Harry dropped onto the seat. "Can you believe those guys?"

Tony gazed at him in silence for a moment, before bursting into laughter.

Harry gaped at him. "What's so funny?"

It took Tony a minute or two to get himself under control. "You've got yourself a fan club there."

"Me?"

Tony stared at him. "You have no idea, do you?" He took a long drink from his glass.

"Why would they be interested in me?" Harry didn't get it. Of the two of them, Tony was the freaking *gorgeous* one, tall, tanned, with jeans that hugged his long legs, stunning dark eyes, toned upper arms…

Tony put down his glass. "Harry, we're in a gay bar that usually draws guys of a particular type. No twinks here, just beards, muscles, big guys…. You know, the kind of guy you see in the mirror every day." His eyes shone. "Now me? I wouldn't get a look-in with most of the men downstairs. The age is right, but babe, when it comes to what they like in a guy?" He reached over and stroked Harry's thigh. "*You* are it."

"But I'm not—"

Tony stopped his words with a kiss, and Harry was more than happy to go with that. When they parted, Tony indicated the small couch that faced them, where two guys were sprawled, their arms around each other. Big, burly guys, one with a full beard, the other in a leather vest that revealed a thick layer of chest hair.

Both men were smiling at Harry.

Tony leaned in, his lips brushing Harry's earlobe. "And before you tell me *again* that you're not good-looking, take a gander at their expressions," he whispered. "Because given half a chance? Those two would be up for anything with you. They see a fucking beautiful bear." Tony shifted until he looked Harry in the eye. "Which is exactly what I see." Then he gave a gleeful grin. "Unfortunately for them, they're not gonna get their mitts on you, because tonight, sexy, you're all mine. And when we've had a couple of pints, we're gonna get our dancing shoes on."

Harry raised his eyebrows. "Where, exactly?" His dancing days had been a long time ago.

Tony got out his phone and scrolled down the screen. "There." He held it out for Harry to see.

Harry was trying hard not to snicker. "Beefmince? Where is it, in an abattoir?"

"You'll see when we get there." Tony put his phone away. "Now drink your pint, and try not to let the lustful stares put you off."

Harry picked up his glass, shaking his head. The evening's events kept on surprising him at every turn. He had no clue what to expect next.

Harry had no idea whether he was scared or exhilarated.

Chapter Ten

Tony waited as Harry climbed out of the Uber. "Have you been here before?" The pavement was full of men smoking and talking, and music boomed from inside the Royal Vauxhall Tavern, growing louder when the door opened to admit more patrons. Tony smiled to himself. All in all, a typical Friday night.

Harry frowned. "No, but I've heard of it. I thought you said we were going to some place called Beefmince?"

"Which is what happens here every third Friday of the month." Tony gave a contented sigh. "We're talking beards, bears and cubs—oh my. Not to mention music and booze. Everything you could wish for."

Harry looked a little doubtful, so Tony put his arm around him. "You had a good time at the Duke of Wellington, didn't you?" When Harry nodded, Tony suppressed his sigh of relief. "Well then, this is just like the Duke, only with a lot more guys, louder music, and hot, sweaty bodies on the dance floor."

Harry rolled his eyes. "When you put it like that…"

Tony laughed, his hand still at Harry's back, and guided him to the door where two bouncers were letting guys in and out.

"You got tickets?" the female bouncer asked.

Tony held them up. She stood aside to let them enter, handing over two wristbands.

"When did you get those?" Harry asked loudly.

"Monday night when I left you," Tony told him with a grin. "I wasn't gonna chance them getting full up."

There was a queue at the bar three guys deep, and two hunks were on the stage, gyrating to the beat that pulsed through the floor and walls. Men filled every available space, in various stages of undress, and Tony pushed aside the urge to stare. Okay, so there were some glorious specimens of bearkind out there, but none of them compared to the gorgeous guy at his side.

A guy who was on the receiving end of a *lot* of attention, and he'd only just walked through the frigging door.

Tony tugged his arm. "Drink?"

Harry nodded. "Let me get these?" He seemed anxious to get away from a tall man with a red bandanna tied around his head, a long, thick black beard, and a chest full of vivid tattoos. When Tony moved closer, Harry expelled a long breath. "I don't remember guys being this… up-front about stuff." He indicated the bandanna guy with a flick of his head. "He wasn't in the least bit subtle."

Tony laughed. "I can imagine. Want me to stick close by?" Like he had *any* intention of leaving Harry's side that night. And judging by Harry's enthusiastic nodding, he was more than happy with that idea.

"That barman is trying to get me drunk," Harry told Tony as he deposited two glasses on the small ledge behind them. All around them, guys were in a constant state of motion, moving to the music. Lights pulsed in time to the rhythm, shining on bald heads and bare chests. He saw guys whose facial and body hair more than made up for what was lacking on their heads. Harry had never been in a place with so many hairy guys before. He saw men of thirty and over, with thick, muscled arms, solid bellies, a whole lot of hairy chests...

Men who kept smiling at him. Talking to him. Coming on to him.

Harry still thought he was dreaming.

Tony snorted. "Isn't that what barmen are supposed to do?"

"I'm serious. Every time I go to buy a drink, he gives me a shot of tequila." Then there was the way the barman accidentally on purpose stroked his hand every time Harry paid him. The tequila was definitely loosening him up: he wasn't drunk yet—tipsy was probably a better description. And apart from the fact that he was getting an awful lot of attention, Harry was having a great time.

"Back in a sec." Tony gestured toward the toilets, and Harry nodded in acknowledgment. It was only when Tony had gone that he realized one guy was standing a lot closer.

"I haven't seen you here before," the man said loudly.

Harry gave him a polite look. "First time."

He drank some more of his rum and coke, gazing at the floor show. Two guys in their fifties, with thick, grey beards, were dancing together, both in jeans and black leather braces, arms locked around each other. The way they looked at each other, as if only they existed in that place, sent a shiver down Harry's spine.

"I think you need to come here more often."

It took Harry a moment to realize he was the one being addressed. The guy wore a black and blue plaid shirt, open, revealing a forest covering his chest. A big guy, who was moving closer to Harry, until maybe an inch separated them.

"That's the plan." Tony was at Harry's side, his arm going around his waist. Tony gave the guy an apologetic smile. "But unfortunately for you, this one is mine, so hands off."

God, the relief that swept through him. Harry leaned into Tony, and gave the guy an apologetic smile. "Definitely his." His admirer gave a good-natured shrug and went back to dancing.

Tony regarded him with arched eyebrows. "I can't even leave you alone for five minutes, can I?" He gestured toward the departing admirer, his eyes sparkling with humour. "He was nice."

Harry couldn't help himself. "Maybe, but he wasn't you."

Tony shifted closer, until they were pressed up against each other. "Love how you dance," he said huskily, his body undulating sensually, his arms looped around Harry's neck.

Harry loved the way Tony danced too, the way their bodies connected, the closeness, the heat between them, around them, the music throbbing through the soles of his feet. He lost himself in the rhythm and matched Tony's movements, their gazes locked on each other, the colourful lights playing over them in a riotous dance. Tony rocked against him, and Harry was suddenly aware of hardness hidden in Tony's sinfully tight jeans, a hardness easily matched by his own. The rest of the men dancing around them melted away, until it was just them, just the music, the lights, and the feel of their bodies moving together.

Harry had no idea how long they danced like that. He only knew that it came to an end all too soon.

Tony flashed him a grin. "Time for another drink."

Harry nodded in agreement, only this time, he went with Tony to the bar. They managed to find a space to stand, and Harry took a long swig of his beer. Dancing with Tony had been... hot, and Harry felt younger than he had in years.

"So, wanna tell me what had your knickers in a twist this week?"

Harry frowned. "What do you mean?"

"That night when you came out of work, looking like you were carrying the weight of the world on your shoulders. Was it just a bad day?"

The penny dropped. "Ah, right. We got a new bloke at the office, and let's just say he might be a problem child."

Tony raised his eyebrows. "Really?" Harry relayed Simon's antics without mentioning any names. When he'd finished, Tony's stare hadn't diminished. "Can I ask something? Why didn't you read him the riot act? 'Cause it sounds like he bloody deserved it."

Harry shook his head. "That's not my style.

Besides, he's new, finding his feet. I have no idea what issues he has, but laying into him wouldn't have helped matters. Now if he'd continued, then sure, I'd have said something, but being all heavy-handed right off the bat isn't the way to get the best out of people."

Tony stared at him in silence for a moment, until Harry felt a little awkward. Then Tony smiled, and Harry got the impression that something had changed. What, he wasn't exactly sure, but it was definitely a positive thing.

Tony gestured toward the floor where guys were still dancing. "Had enough? Do you want to go home? Or maybe you want another shot of tequila from the hot guy behind the bar who's been eyeing you up since you walked in." His grin widened.

Harry knew exactly what he wanted, and it certainly wasn't the hot barman. "Let's see where the nearest Uber is."

Tony's phone was out a second later, but as he scrolled, Harry stilled his hand. "You're coming home with me, right?"

Tony's only response was a slow, lingering kiss that had Harry wanting more. Tony pulled back, his breathing quickening. "Now give me a sec to find an Uber?" He returned his attention to his phone. Harry took advantage of his occupied state to stand behind him, his arms around Tony's waist as he nuzzled Tony's neck.

"Christ," Tony muttered. "Can't think when you do that."

His words did more for Harry than all the appreciative glances he'd received all night.

"Okay, the Uber will be here in about twenty minutes."

Harry beamed. "Time for another drink then." He grabbed hold of Tony's hand and tugged him toward the bar. "And you're coming with me as back-up."

Tony laughed. "This my new job? Harry's bodyguard?"

Harry was definitely feeling merry. "We'll see when we get back to my place. You'll have to pass the interview first."

And that'll be in my bed.

Harry didn't want to wait anymore.

"This is becoming a habit," Tony said as they closed the front door behind them. "Me seeing you home when you've had a skinful." He snickered. "Are you trying to tell me something? Like, the only way to spend an evening with me is to get drunk?"

Harry kicked off his shoes. "'M not drunk. An' *you* were the one who wanted to go for a drink, r'member?" Then before Tony could reply, he lurched at him, pinning him against the wall in his hallway, locking lips in a kiss that Tony lost no time in returning. Tony's hands were everywhere, on his shoulders, his back, his arse. Harry thrust his tongue deep into Tony's mouth, loving the moan that burst out of him.

"Upstairs," Harry gasped out, breaking the breathless kiss long enough to grab Tony's hand and tug him up the staircase. No sooner were they through his bedroom door, than they both tumbled onto the bed, Harry on top of Tony, kissing his neck and mouth, while Tony's fingers were in his hair, on his nape, before sliding down his body to grab hold of his arse and squeeze hard.

Harry sought the buttons on Tony's shirt, fumbling as he tried to undo them.

"Fuck, gimme a chance to get my breath." Tony's short laugh was a joyous sound. Harry paused in his task to move his hand lower, cupping the bulge in Tony's jeans.

To his surprise, Tony circled Harry's wrist with his fingers, stopping him. "Hey," he said softly, his breathing rapid.

Harry stared at him. "What's wrong?"

Tony sighed. "We're not gonna do this. Not like this, anyway."

"What the fuck?" Harry rolled off him and knelt on the bed. "I don't see a problem. You're here, and—"

"And now I've got some oxygen to my brain, I'm thinking a little more clearly." Tony's gaze met his. "I'm not about to take advantage of you, Harry."

Harry blinked. "Take—" He grabbed Tony's hand and brought it to his own crotch. "And if I *want* you to take advantage? What then?" He swallowed. "I want you," he whispered.

Tony pulled his hand away, sat up, and locked his arms around Harry's neck. "And I want you too. Fuck, I want you. But… when we have sex for the first time, I want you sober. I want you to remember every second of it."

Harry flopped down onto the bed, throwing his arm over his face. His body tingled and his dick ached, but deep down he knew what Tony said was right.

He didn't have to like it though.

Tony's hand was warm on his thigh. "You need to sleep, okay?" The bed dipped as he shifted closer. "And it's not like I'm saying it's not gonna happen. Just… not right this second."

"Sure." Harry rolled onto his side, facing away from Tony. His head was in a mess. *Maybe he's just saying that because he's trying to be kind.* Except that didn't make sense. Tony's mouth on his, the way he'd touched Harry… he'd wanted this as much as Harry did. There was no faking the desire he'd seen in Tony's eyes.

And maybe he's right, and I'm not sober enough to think straight.

Then sleep took him.

It didn't take Harry more than two seconds to realize that what had awoken him in the middle of the night was the dire need to pee. What surprised the hell out of him, however, was the warm arm draped over him, the warm body pressed up against his back.

He stayed.

Then Harry realized he was no longer dressed, and judging by the feel of Tony's chest against his back, neither was Tony. *He undressed me again?* This was getting to be a habit.

Harry's bladder stopped any more such thoughts, and he eased himself out of bed, crept out of the room and across the small landing into the toilet. When he'd finished, he crept into the bathroom to run water quickly over his hands, then went back to the bedroom. Carefully he got back into bed, putting some distance between himself and Tony. He hadn't been there but five minutes, before Tony made a small noise and shifted across the mattress, as if he was seeking Harry in his sleep. Harry caught his breath when Tony snuggled up behind him once more, his arm coming around Harry to hold him close. Tony let out a sigh and seconds later, his breathing changed as he slipped into a deeper sleep.

There seemed to be no getting away from Tony when he was asleep any more than when he was awake. Then it struck Harry that maybe this was a good thing.

Harry closed his eyes, hoping that when he opened them, Tony would still be there.

Chapter Eleven

Harry's first thought on waking was that his head wasn't pounding as much as he thought it would be. Obviously, he hadn't been *that* drunk the previous night. His next was that the bed was way too empty.

No Tony. *Well shit.*

Not that deep down, Harry wasn't surprised, but what overwhelmed him most was a feeling of disappointment. He'd really hoped…

When the sound of cheerful whistling greeted his ears, he froze. *Well, what do you know?* A wave of bright joy rolled over him, and he sat up quickly, running a hand over his bed hair, just as Tony came through the door, wearing only his jeans and carrying a tray containing two steaming mugs and what was unmistakably hot buttered toast.

Bloody hell. Yet again, Tony's jeans were unfastened, revealing just enough of his pubes to have Harry's dick stiffening below the sheets. Before he could comment on this, however, Tony gave him a firm stare.

"We really need to talk."

Harry's stomach clenched. "We do?"

Tony's eyes suddenly held a twinkle that eased Harry's fears. "Instant coffee? Are you kidding me? What's with that shit? Mate, you really need to get some decent coffee." He gave a slow, sexy grin. "If I'm gonna be staying over here more often, then I'm getting you a cafetière and some good ground coffee."

Harry wasn't sure whether he was pissed off at the reaction to his usual beverage, startled by the announcement that Tony was considering staying more, or annoyed at his presumption that he needed to provide Harry with the necessary equipment to make *his* stay more comfortable. The smell of the toast proved the deciding factor.

"Insulting my coffee will *not* get you another invitation to stay, you know." He levelled a hard stare in Tony's direction, but it was difficult to maintain the pretence, not when Tony stood there looking so… fucking *gorgeous*. Harry gestured to the toast. "You needn't have gone to all this trouble."

"It's no trouble. I wanted to surprise you. Although my choices for breakfast in bed were limited by the contents of your fridge." That familiar grin made another appearance. "I gather shopping is on your list of things to do this weekend: you've got nothing in, have you?"

Shit. The last thing Harry wanted was Tony poking around in his fridge. It wasn't as if he cooked anyway—his meals were usually of the takeaway or 'shove in the microwave and ping' variety. And since he'd been cutting down on food…

"You're right. Actually, I do have a lot of stuff to get through this weekend. I'd… better get started, yeah?" And without giving Tony time to respond, Harry dove out from beneath the sheets and zipped out of the room, heading for the bathroom. Once inside, he leaned against the door, his heart pounding. He knew he was being an arse, but the last thing he wanted was Tony asking awkward questions. Harry had a feeling Tony wouldn't approve of his new regime. Then it occurred to him that Tony's opinion mattered.

Harry pulled the cord to start the water heating, then reached in through the shower curtain to flip on the water, waiting while it got past the initial freezing-his-balls-off stage. He climbed into the tight enclosure, bowed his head, and let the water cascade down his body. The shower had been his dad's brainwave, not that there was really enough space for it in the tiny bathroom: he'd taken out the linen shelves, tiled the walls, and called in a plumber to do the rest.

Harry lost himself in the feel of hot water on his skin, the glide of a soapy hand over his body—until the shower curtain moved, and a very naked Tony stepped into the space.

"Ooh, cosy."

Harry was too shocked to respond. He backed into the corner, his heart pounding as Tony maneuvered himself carefully onto his knees in front of him, his eyes level with Harry's dick—that was definitely taking an interest in the proceedings.

Tony looked up at him. "This is for me, right?"

Harry swallowed, his throat tight. Then he closed his eyes as Tony took the head of his cock into wet heat. "Oh fuck," he moaned weakly. His leg twitched, and Tony laid a gentle hand on his thigh, before pulling free of his dick and stroking Harry's leg.

"Easy, babe," he whispered. Tony leaned in and kissed the swell of Harry's belly, soft kisses that moved in a southerly direction, until he was right back where Harry wanted him, holding Harry's cock upright with a single finger while he leisurely licked up its length. Harry shuddered as Tony sucked hard on the head, then let out a low groan when Tony took him deep.

"Oh my God, that's...." Harry planted his hands on Tony's head, keeping him there, his dick buried in Tony's throat. When Tony pulled back, red-faced and grinning, saliva dripping from his lips and Harry's shaft, Harry guided him back, thrusting, his hips rolling as he drove his cock into that wonderful mouth. Fuck, when was the last time he'd enjoyed a guy's mouth on him? Water poured down, hitting Tony's body, and still Tony kept on sliding his lips along Harry's shaft, until his nose was buried in Harry's pubes, his hands stroking over Harry's belly, slow and sensual.

"Tony... getting close," Harry gasped out.

Tony proceeded to move faster, his head bobbing. He kept one hand on Harry's belly, and with the other, he started pumping his own cock, the pace frenetic. Harry stiffened as that glorious sensation coursed through him, all the way down to his balls, and he shot his load down Tony's throat. Warmth spattered against his calf, and he knew Tony had come too. Tony licked and sucked the head of his dick, slowing in his movements, until he resumed the leisurely tongue bath that had started the proceedings.

When not a drop remained, Tony sat back on his haunches and sighed contentedly. "Now *that's* the way to wake up." He got to his feet and reached for the lemon bodywash on the small shelf above his head. "And now I get to touch this gorgeous body some more."

Before Harry could say a word, Tony

squeezed the liquid into his palm, worked it into a lather, and rubbed his hands unhurriedly over Harry's chest and stomach. Harry couldn't help his reaction: he leaned in and kissed Tony softly on the lips, tasting his own come there. Tony moved sensually against him, their bodies slippery, their cocks sliding against each other.

When Tony finally came to a halt, he broke the kiss with a happy sigh. "Thank you."

Harry snickered. "I think I'm the one who should be thanking you."

Tony smiled. "Nah. I invited myself in here, didn't I? You could have told me to sling me hook."

Harry snorted. "Yeah, right. Like I'd turn down the chance of a morning blow job." He flipped off the water and gestured toward the curtain. "Use the towel on the rail. I'll get another." He pulled the curtain aside and stepped out onto the bathmat. Another towel hung on the hook behind the door, and he grabbed that, hastily wrapping it around himself as he left the bathroom in a hurry. He had no idea why he was overcome with embarrassment. Perhaps it was simply the length of time that had passed since he'd last had sex. There was no denying Tony had felt amazing, however.

By the time Harry had pulled on his jeans, Tony was back in his bedroom, rubbing his hair dry with the towel. "Did you say something about going shopping?"

Harry froze. "Yes. Why?"

"Well, I thought I might come along. I sort of wanted to cook dinner for you this evening, so I could put together a list and…" Tony stared at him. "Why am I getting the feeling that you don't like that idea?"

Harry shrugged, although his heart was hammering. "No clue."

Tony's eyes gleamed. "Tell that to your face. Don't you want me to cook for you? Is that it?"

Harry had the uncomfortable sensation that Tony was steamrollering his way into every aspect of Harry's life. He'd already noted the lack of food in the fridge: Harry didn't want him seeing the contents of his shopping basket too.

Tony cleared his throat. "Harry?"

There was no getting away from it.

Harry took a deep breath. "Look, I'm glad you stayed last night, and what... just happened was... amazing, but..."

Tony was standing so still. "There's a but?"

Harry bit the bullet and plunged ahead. "It just feels like you're bulldozing your way into my life, that's all."

"I see." The hurt on Tony's face was unmistakable, and Harry's heart sank like a boulder. He couldn't help the fact that right then, he felt...vulnerable. It had been hard enough to understand why anyone would like him in the first place, and added to that was the fear of being judged.

It's self-preservation. If Tony was going to walk away anyway—because why the hell would he want to stay with Harry?—then it was going to hurt. Harry would rather push him away then open himself up to that kind of pain or rejection.

"Well, if that's how you feel... maybe I should leave." In silence Tony pulled on his shirt and buttoned it. There was no outward display of emotion, no coolness, just a resignation that filled Harry with sorrow.

It was like watching a car crash, unable to stop it from happening. Harry's stomach clenched, his throat tight. When Tony was dressed, he stood beside the bed, his features neutral.

God, so much for avoiding pain. This fucking *hurt*.

"I guess I'll see you on Monday morning when you pass me on your way to work," Tony said simply. "Don't bother to see me out. I know the way, right?" And with that, he left the room. Harry listened to the sound of his feet on the stairs, followed by the dull thud of the front door closing behind him.

He sank onto the bed, his head in his hands.

When you fuck things up, you really *fuck things up.*

Chapter Twelve

It seemed to Harry that his thoughts were on a permanent default all day Sunday.

He couldn't stop thinking about Tony.

He'd spent a miserable night, getting little sleep, and when he finally climbed out of bed, bleary-eyed and fatigued, breakfast was the last thing he wanted. He drank a couple of mugs of coffee, and the sight of the jar only served to remind him. Harry had done his grocery shopping the previous day—what there was of it—and he'd paused at the shelf containing bags of ground coffee.

Then he'd given himself a shake. Why bother? What if Tony never came back?

That had only brought more misery.

Sunday lunchtime came and went, and Harry told himself he didn't need the calories. Only this time, there was that small, nagging voice at the back of his mind. Tony hadn't minded the way Harry looked in the shower, had he? Quite the opposite. Yet in spite of all the attention Harry had received Friday evening, he was still at a loss to understand why Tony was interested in him. That only made him think about all the good-looking men who'd gazed at him. What did they see that *he* didn't? They couldn't *all* need glasses.

Harry wanted to kick himself. Why was it he found it so difficult to believe Tony—or any of the guys at the bar—would be interested in him? He'd gain a little self-confidence, then revert to his original pattern of thinking.

His laptop sat on the coffee table, and Harry regarded it with interest.

Maybe a little research was called for.

He switched it on, and typed a couple of words into the search engine: gay bears. It didn't take long for the results to appear, and Harry was staggered by what he saw. Photos. Websites just for bears. Picture after picture of men who looked astoundingly like him, the same build, same amount of body hair.

When he pulled up porn sites, it got a lot more interesting. There were entire sites dedicated to bears having sex, with twinky guys, with each other…

Is that how Tony sees me?

What came to mind was the way Tony had caressed his belly while he'd sucked Harry's dick, the movement gentle and sensual. Maybe losing a ton of weight wasn't such a good idea.

It was enough to push him into making dinner, albeit a smaller portion than usual. Nothing wrong with keeping an eye on his weight, right?

By the time evening arrived, Harry was still thinking about Tony. He had no clue how he was going to react the following morning when he saw Tony at the site. The memory of the hurt etched on Tony's face hadn't left him.

Maybe I'll play it by ear. Maybe Tony will act differently. Maybe I've put him off.

That last thought brought a wave of dismay so acute, that Harry's chest ached.

God, I hope not.

"Tony. Tony!" Ben's voice finally penetrated.

Tony tore his gaze away from the street below, viewed through the space where a window would eventually go, and turned reluctantly. "Yeah?"

Ben gave him a lopsided grin. "If it's not too much trouble, d'you think you might actually do some work this morning? I mean, unless you've something more pressing to do."

"He's probably still knackered from 'is weekend," Steve said with a cackle. "Shagging takes a lot of energy, right?"

Tony didn't even bother to dignify that remark with a response. "Sorry," he murmured to Ben, before packing more insulation in between the wall studs. The outer skin of the new apartment block was done: all that was needed were the windows, and the doors that opened up onto small balconies. A bus rumbled by, which had him whipping his head around so fast, he got a crick in his neck. Tony dashed over to the window space and peered out. Sure enough, a moment later Harry came into view, his gait stiff, his gaze locked on the street ahead.

Come on, Harry. Look at me. Look at me.

It wasn't until the last minute that Harry turned his head in Tony's direction. After a moment's scanning, he gave Tony a brief nod. Then he was gone.

At least I got that much. Tony hadn't gotten

much sleep the previous two nights. He'd longed to call Harry on Sunday, but every time he picked up his phone, at the last minute he'd changed his mind and tossed it aside. *If he wants to talk to me, he knows my number.* Except Tony knew it was a cop-out.

He didn't want to call, only to be told Harry wanted nothing more to do with him.

"You two had a row or something?" Ben asked quietly. "Because I couldn't help noticing…"

Tony walked through the door space to the scaffolding platform beyond, safely out of earshot of the others, and Ben joined him. Tony leaned on the rail and sighed. "I just don't get him. It's like… when Harry looks in a mirror, the image he sees is distorted. He doesn't see what me and the rest of the bleeding world sees."

"None of us do that, mate," Ben replied.

"Yeah, but I really thought I'd gotten through to him after Beefmince."

Ben blinked. "What the 'ell is—on second thoughts, forget I asked. I don't wanna know." He inclined his head in the direction of Harry's office. "Would it help if you went an' talked to him?"

Right then, Tony wasn't sure. "I'm just gonna leave him alone for a few days. Maybe that's best."

"Fine. But don't let this go on too long," Ben admonished. "'Cause even a straight idiot like me can see you like each other."

Tony gave his mate a warm glance. "Since when are you an idiot? Okay, I can overlook the fact that you're straight, 'cause nobody's perfect." He took a deep breath. "I'll give him until Wednesday. If things haven't changed by then, maybe I'll say something." He inclined his head toward the pile of insulation sheets. "Okay you, back to work. These won't fit themselves, y'know. And we *are* here to work, remember?"

Then he nimbly dodged Ben's playful lunge and scooted back across the boarded surface to carry on working.

Come on, Harry. We're good together. Don't let's lose that.

Wednesday evening, Harry locked up the office and began the trek to the bus stop, his stomach churning the same way it had been for the last three days. He'd given only the most perfunctory nods in Tony's direction as he'd passed the site, not waiting to see if Tony acknowledged them. The sense of shame hadn't left him, and the more he thought about it, the more his shame deepened. So what if Tony had wanted to cook dinner for him? It wasn't as if he'd started making lists for wedding invitations, right? Harry knew he'd overreacted, but making the first move was proving more difficult than he'd anticipated.

As he drew closer to the site, he realized Tony had given up waiting for him to be the bigger man.

He was leaning against the fence, his work bag at his feet. What made the view all the more enticing was the sight of Tony's bare, tanned chest, framed by his open denim jacket. Where it clung to Tony's biceps, however, his muscles strained the seams as the sleeves emphasized every swell and curve.

Fuck, that's sexy.

Tony's gaze was focused on Harry.

No backing out now.

What sent a shiver down his spine was the absence of Tony's habitual smile.

He pushed off the fence and straightened, hands still stuffed in the pockets of his jeans. "Hi."

Harry came to a halt in front of Tony and simply gave a nod in reply, his throat dry.

Tony gave him an inquiring glance. "So… what's going on? I haven't seen much of you this past week."

He could have made an excuse, but he didn't. "Yeah, I'm sorry. And there's not been much going on."

"Except the fact that you've been avoiding me." Tony moved closer, until Harry could smell the woodsy cologne that had clung to his pillow since Saturday night. "So I decided enough was enough."

Harry's heartbeat quickened, along with his breathing. "Oh?" It was as he'd feared. Tony had run out of patience. He'd finally realized what a mistake he'd made. He'd—

"I'm not giving up on you, Harry." Tony's voice was barely a whisper. "You got that?"

Not giving up on me. Whatever else Harry thought was lost when Tony leaned in and kissed him, softly at first, then deeper, his hands snaking around Harry's waist, holding onto him.

Harry forgot his shame, his regret, and lost himself in that kiss, his heart soaring.

When they parted, Tony locked gazes with him. "No more avoiding me," he said quietly.

"Okay? I'm not going anywhere, so you'd better get used to the idea." His smile sent a flush of warmth through Harry. "Now let's get a few things straight. If you want me to stay at your place, just ask. If you *don't* want me there, you let me know that too. We'll play this by whatever rules make you comfortable."

God, Harry liked the sound of that.

"Yes," he breathed, before dropping his bag to the ground, taking Tony's face in his hands and kissing him with more enthusiasm than before. *I missed this.*

Tony broke the kiss, laughing. "Wow. If this is what a few days' absence does, I may need to do this more often." He cocked his head to one side. "So… what do you want to do tonight?"

"Would it be okay if I just went home?" Harry wanted to get started on his housecleaning.

He had an idea his weekend would be busy with other activities.

Tony waved his hand. "Like I said. Whatever makes you comfortable."

Harry stroked his cheek. "But this weekend… want to do something?"

Tony's face lit up. "You bet."

And with that, the weight of the past few days rolled away, leaving Harry feeling lighter.

I'm not pushing him away again.

Then Tony's arms tightened around him again. "One more hug for the road?"

Harry laughed. "Like you need an excuse." He held Tony close, breathing him in—and freezing when a low sound caught his ears. "What was that?" He took a step back.

"What was what?"

Harry peered toward the fence, from where

the sound came. A large cardboard box sat against the fence, and—

"That box just moved."

Tony turned to look. "What the hell?"

The box shifted a little, and a plaintive mewl emerged from it. Harry dashed over and knelt beside it, opening it. Inside was a kitten, gazing up at him with liquid eyes. It was black, with a little white star-shaped mark on its chest, and it was staring at Harry the way only kittens can, with an adorable expression that melted the heart.

Tony joined him, kneeling too. "Aww. What lowlife sticks a kitten in a cardboard box and just leaves it?"

"Did you notice anyone here today?" Harry took one look at the kitten who stretched up on its hind legs and tried to touch him with its tiny front paws, mewing pitifully, and he was lost.

Tony shook his head. "I've been indoors all day. Wouldn't have seen a thing."

Harry reached into the box and scooped up the kitten. It was so small, it sat in one hand. "Hey, little…." He carefully turned it over to peer at the kitten's undercarriage. "Girl. Aren't you sweet?"

Tony stroked the kitten along her back, and Harry felt the purr that vibrated through her little body. "She's a cute one." He sat back on his haunches. "So what are you going to do with her?"

"Me?" Harry blinked.

Tony huffed. "Well, I can't take her. Mum would have a shit fit. Besides, she's allergic."

Harry thought fast. "There's a vet on Lower Addiscombe road, near my place. I'll take her there to get checked out."

"Mm-hmm. Well, it stands to reason that no

one is gonna claim her, not if they abandoned her like this. What are you gonna do once she's checked out?"

Harry would think about that particular hurdle when it appeared. Right then he had a kitten to consider. He gently placed it back into the box, and the kitten stood up on its small back legs and placed a paw on his hand, mewling softly.

Harry's heart melted all over again.

Tony stared at him. "I think I know you, and then you go and surprise me."

Harry carefully eased the kitten back into the box and closed the flaps. "A good surprise?"

Tony's eyes shone. "Definitely." He rose to his feet. "And I'm coming with you. So let's go."

Harry lifted the box into the air, and Tony grabbed both their bags.

His evening had taken an unexpected turn, and Harry couldn't have been happier about it.

Chapter Thirteen

"Well, good morning, gorgeous." Tony leered at him from the fence.

Harry tried to affect a stern expression, but he knew it would be an epic fail. "I swear this is exactly where we were last evening. Shouldn't you be working, instead of waiting to accost unwary members of the public?"

Tony gave him a cheerful grin. "But you're not a member of the public. You're my fella." He paused, as if waiting for Harry to protest, or deny it, or something.

Harry knew a good thing when it was leaning against a fence, looking bloody hot in denim. "Yeah, I am," he said softly. What use was there in denying something he wanted so badly?

His words seemed to flick a switch in Tony, who straightened, walked over to him, and kissed him gently on the lips. "Well, Hallelujah," he said, his eyes shining. "My day just got a whole lot better." He gave Harry another quick kiss. "But you're right. I do need to crack on with work. I'll meet you here this evening and we can discuss how we're going to spend the weekend."

Harry beamed. "Shopping done, housework done... I'm all yours."

Tony groaned. "You're not helping, y'know." When Harry gave him a quizzical glance, Tony widened his gaze. "There I am, all ready to go back over there and slave over a hot saw, and you tell me you're all mine. Kind of makes me wish it was Saturday already." He slipped his arms around Harry and squeezed his behind. "God, your arse feels good in these. Although, now I know what it feels like when it's just you, wet—"

"And you can stop right there." How Harry kept his voice firm, he'd never know. "Work, mister." Work was the perfect thing to cool his stiffening dick in its tracks.

Tony rolled his eyes. "Spoilsport." He let go of Harry. "Now tell me you've not been thinking about that little kitten all night."

Harry laughed. "No, I haven't. Because right now she's spending time with the vet. And no, I'm not going out and buying a pet bowl and other accessories, because she's not mine, okay?"

Tony snickered. "Yeah, right. Keep telling yourself that." He headed for the gate in the fence, waving a hand. "Later."

Harry took advantage of his retreat to ogle that arse and those firm thighs from behind.

My fella. It still didn't feel real.

So what? Harry told himself belligerently. *Make the most of it.* Then he smiled to himself. Tony had nailed him on one thing: he'd been thinking about the kitten all right.

When he got to the office, Simon was already there, shuffling from one foot to the other. He stubbed out his cigarette on the pavement as Harry approached. "Morning, boss," he said brightly.

Harry did a quick reckoning. Deb would be the next to arrive, but he had about ten minutes before that to have a little chat with his latest staff member. "Morning." He got out the keys and unlocked the main door. "Why don't you get the coffee machine going, then come over to my desk and we'll have a talk."

Simon arched his eyebrows. "Sounds… intriguing." He put his bag down on his chair and walked toward the kitchen.

Harry went over to his desk, placed his bag in the roomy bottom drawer, then sat down. He'd been thinking about Simon during the past week, and figured it was time to find out what was going on.

Simon sauntered over, pulled a chair up to Harry's desk and dropped into it. "Coffee's on. So… what are we talking about?"

Harry leaned back. "Are you settling in all right?" It was a fairly innocuous conversation opener, but he wasn't about to launch right into what he'd planned.

Simon shrugged. "S'ppose."

"I only ask because you made one hell of an entrance. I think you'd been here a day before you'd put someone's back up." He kept his tone light.

Simon let out a dramatic sigh. "That's me. They either love me or hate me. I'm adorbs or I'm a turd. No in-between."

Harry eyed him speculatively. "Yes, well, I'd believe that, if you hadn't appeared to go out of your way to get in someone's face. And that's putting it politely."

"Someone been telling tales?" Simon's eyes glittered. He didn't seem overly concerned. If anything, he appeared… pleased.

Harry widened his stare. "Hardly surprising, I'd say, not after the way you behaved. So I have to ask myself, why would someone starting a new job go out of their way to aggravate his colleagues? Because no one acts the way you did without a reason."

Simon bit his lip, and just like that, the camp facade slipped away. What struck Harry in that moment was how young he seemed. Then reality hit him. Simon was only twenty—that *was* young. Not that thirty-five was ancient. In fact, lately, Harry had been feeling decidedly younger.

How does that saying go? You're only as old as the man you feel? That made him smile.

"Can I be honest?"

Harry gave him a reassuring smile. "I'd prefer that."

Simon regarded him in silence for a moment. "When my last manager told me they were moving me to the Croydon branch, I was pissed off. I wanted something more… central. I mean, Croydon?" He rolled his eyes. "I wanted someplace where I could leave the office and be in a club within minutes. So… I thought that if I made a big enough stink, you'd transfer me."

Harry tried not to laugh. "Are you that naive?"

"What do you mean?"

Apparently, he was. "You haven't been working all that long, have you? You really thought that by acting up, they'd send you where you wanted to be in the first place? Business doesn't work like that. Head office would be more inclined to discipline you, and then send you to some god-awful hole in the back of beyond, just to make sure you learned your lesson."

Simon stilled. "You serious?"

Harry nodded. "And all this flamboyant behaviour, coming on to Ron… really? What was that, 'Look at me, I'm gay?' If you were trying to shock, I'm sorry to break it to you, but you're *not* the only gay in the village. And Ron might be the sweetest guy, but you can only push him so far. You were lucky you didn't get your lights punched out."

Simon sagged into the chair. "Are you going to write this up? I mean, does Head Office have to know about it?"

Harry shook his head. "We'll keep this between us, with the proviso that you get on with your job and your colleagues. How does that sound?"

Simon nodded eagerly. "Sounds cool."

Harry couldn't resist. "Although I should tell you... it's not such a good idea to come onto the builders on the site next door. That is a really good way to make sure you get your head kicked in, because as far as I know, only one of them is gay, and he's spoken for." Harry beamed.

"And how would you know that, unless..." Simon's eyes widened. "Ooh get you. Nice one." Then he winked. "I don't know, though. Wanna know what it takes to turn a straight man gay?" He grinned. "Tequila."

Harry laughed. "You live way too dangerously." He had a job to do, however, and it was time to set aside levity. "But to put things into perspective? Your behaviour should have resulted in you either getting fired, or never being able to rise to a position of responsibility. The fact that it didn't is purely down to you having a boss who doesn't want to blight a promising career. You work well, Simon. Don't spoil that."

Simon pushed out a sigh that sounded very much like relief. "Thanks, Mr. Forrest."

Harry cleared his throat. "I think we've

moved on to Harry by now. Especially if we're discussing my boyfriend." Damn, that felt good to say.

Simon appeared pleased. "Okay… Harry. And seriously? You have good taste. A builder? Which one, by the way?"

It wasn't a conversation Harry would have indulged in if there had been staff around, but as it was just the two of them…. "The tall streak of gorgeousness usually in Levis."

Simon's jaw dropped. "No shit." When Harry raised his eyebrows, he flushed. "Sorry, but… *niiiice.*"

At that moment, the coffee machine beeped, and the door opened as Deb entered. "Morning, boss," she said brightly. She sniffed the air. "Ooh, nice timing." Deb peered at them sitting together. "Am I interrupting something?" She gave a cheeky grin.

Harry glanced across at Simon and straightened his face. "Yes. We're talking about shoes."

Deb blinked. "Shoes?"

Simon coughed, then adopted a serious expression. "Yeah. I've got this amazing pair of heels that Harry would totally rock."

Harry snorted. "Not with these legs."

Simon snickered. "I'll get you a coffee, boss." He got up from his chair and left the room.

Deb stared at Harry. "You know what? I think 'avin' Simon 'ere has been good for you."

Harry knew the change in him was nothing to do with Simon, and *everything* to do with a certain hunky guy who was a mere stone's throw away.

A guy who'd be sharing Harry's weekend.

And judging by what had happened the previous weekend, Harry thought it might be time to shop for supplies. He couldn't remember the last time he'd bought condoms, but he was certain any remaining in his bedside drawer were *long* past their Use By date. The idea sent a thrill of anticipation skittering through him.

He couldn't wait to see what happened next.

As soon as he got close enough to see Tony's face, Harry knew something was wrong. "Hey."

Tony gave a half-smile. "Hiya." He joined Harry, and slowly they walked toward the bus stop. When a minute or two had gone by, and Tony hadn't said a word, Harry plunged ahead.

"Okay, what's wrong?"

"My bleedin' Aunt Rosa, that's what happened," Tony said morosely. "I got a call from Mum about ten minutes ago. Aunt Rosa has to fly out to Malaga in the morning, and muggins here is the only person available to take her to the airport." They came to a halt at the stop, and both sat on the seats under the shelter. "She's a nervous flier at the best of times, and usually my cousin would take her, but he's up north on business, so that leaves me."

"I see. How long will it take to drop her off and come back?"

Tony studied his hands. "I have to have her there two hours before the flight, which is at ten-thirty, and it takes roughly forty minutes to get there, depending on traffic. So I'll be leaving her place at around seven-forty-five. When I know she's safely at her gate, I'll come home."

"So we lose a morning. I can deal with that." Harry had no clue what they'd be doing anyway.

Tony stilled, then cocked his head to one side. "Wanna come along for the ride?" His eyes sparkled.

"Really? I mean, how would your aunt feel about that?"

Tony waved a hand. "She'll be glad to have someone else in the car to talk to. And believe me, that woman can *talk*. Besides, once we've dropped her off and seen her through Security, we'll have the rest of the day to ourselves."

Something about the gleam in Tony's eye told Harry that Tony might already have an idea of what to do with that day.

Harry was more than happy to go along with whatever Tony had in mind.

"And about tonight…" Tony leaned back against the Perspex bus shelter. "I had intended us going out, but Mum sent me a text saying she had some jobs she wanted doing this weekend. So I thought I'd get 'em done this evening, then we'll have all weekend free." His usually sunny smile slipped a little. "I swear, Tanya has the right idea." Before Harry could inquire as to the meaning of that statement, Tony pointed to a spot over Harry's shoulder. "Here's your bus. Go home, get a good night's sleep, and before you know it, I'll be at your place revoltingly early tomorrow morning." He gave a knowing smile. "I'll bring the coffee."

Harry laughed. "You just want to make sure it's drinkable." He got out his Oyster card, and as the doors opened, he gave Tony a peck on the cheek.

"See you in the morning. And no embarrassing me in front of your aunt."

Tony straightened his features and crossed his heart. "Best behaviour, I promise." Then he grinned. "At least until Auntie Rosa is out of sight. Then all bets are off. And by the way? Wear comfortable shoes for walking in."

Harry had no time to question that statement before the driver coughed loudly. "You gettin' on or what?"

Harry got onto the bus, tapped his card, then sank into the first available seat. As the bus pulled away from the stop, he couldn't miss Tony's grin.

Oh, God. What now?

Chapter Fourteen

It wasn't until he was gazing out of his front window, waiting for Tony's car to appear, that it occurred to Harry he had no idea what Tony drove. He had visions of a beaten up, dusty truck, laden with tools, and his Aunt Rosa perched in the back, clutching a suitcase.

He'd been awake since five and had already drunk two or three mugs of coffee. That had led to him going to the bathroom at least twice, because no way was he going to be caught short during the trip to Gatwick. He'd put on his new jeans, and one of the new T-shirts that Arnold had chosen, then gazed at his reflection. The knowledge that Aunt Rosa would also be there added a little pressure, and he didn't want to let Tony down. He ran a hand over his neatly trimmed beard. The thought had occurred to him to shave it off, but then he recalled Tony's reaction when he'd suggested it.

Harry sighed. When he was in his twenties, anyone with facial hair had just seemed… old, and as for *fancying* a guy with a beard…. Yet there had been any number of men with full beards at the Royal Vauxhall Tavern, and they certainly didn't want for attention. What had surprised him were the guys who were obviously there because they *really* liked bears.

Five minutes later, a horn sounded, and he pulled back the lace curtain. Tony grinned at him from the front seat of an older Mini that was obviously well cared for. The red paintwork gleamed, and the chrome sparkled. Harry hurried to the door, grabbed his bag and jacket, and left the house. He headed for the rear of the car, but Tony gestured for him to join him at the front.

Harry climbed into the seat, dropped his bag at his feet, then was about to fasten his seatbelt when Tony leaned across. "Morning, babe." He kissed Harry's cheek.

A chuckle sounded from the back seat. "Yeah, you were never a shy one."

Harry twisted around to greet Aunt Rosa. She was maybe in her sixties, her once black hair shot with silver, and dark eyes so like Tony's. Her grin was reminiscent of his too. "Hello. I'm Harry." He extended his hand between the seats, and she took it. "And no, shy isn't the first word that *I'd* think of to describe Tony either." Aunt Rosa laughed. Harry glanced around him, noting how far back Tony had pushed the driver's seat. "I think we're gonna need a bigger car."

Tony narrowed his gaze. "Don't you say a word about my girl. I'll have you know, she was my first car."

Harry blinked. "Did you grow taller after you got her? Because you basically have to fold yourself in half to get into her now."

"She was a present from his mum when he passed his test," Aunt Rosa piped up from behind him. "How he fits his tools into that tiny boot, I have no idea."

Tony's mouth fell open. "I'm not puttin' *tools* in her."

Aunt Rosa laughed. "And everyone in the family knows why your mum got you a mini." She leaned forward to speak to Harry. "His dad's favourite film was the Italian Job. Hence the love affair with minis, after watching them tearing through Turin. *Coño*, the number of times Tony begged his mum to let them watch that video."

"Aunt Rosa!" Tony appeared horrified. "You can't say that in front of Harry."

Another laugh escaped her. "Why? Does he speak Spanish? I'll bet he doesn't have a clue what *coño* means."

"And he's not gonna find out either." Before Harry could say a word, Tony glared at him. "So don't ask. And now that my aunt has her mouth under control, if you'll fasten your seatbelt, we can be off. Someone's got a plane to catch, remember?" He glanced over his shoulder to his aunt. "Pass us that mug, please. And best behaviour."

A stainless steel insulated mug appeared from behind him. Harry took it with a smile. "Coffee?"

"Yup. Mum's best morning brew. That'll put hair on your chest—not that you need it." He winked. "You've already got a carpet there."

"I don't need to hear that," Aunt Rosa squeaked. "Can we leave now?"

Tony was still chuckling as he pulled away from the curb. And despite feeling mortified that Tony had said such a thing in front of his elderly aunt, Harry couldn't help smiling.

The journey passed quickly, with Aunt Rosa chatting away about Tony as a little boy, and all the things he'd gotten up to. Harry had the impression that Tony had been a cheeky little boy, with a penchant for sharing whatever was on his mind.

No change there then.

Tony didn't seem to mind her sharing all her tales. He concentrated on his driving, occasionally adding a remark here and there, and only rarely contradicting her. It was clear he and his aunt were close, which didn't surprise Harry in the slightest, after having seen him with his mother and sister. It came as a shock when he saw the overhead signs for the north terminal. It had seemed like no time at all since they'd left his house.

Tony headed for the short stay parking, winding his way up the spiral ramp. Once he'd got his ticket, he found a space and switched off the engine, before twisting around to gaze at his aunt. "Okay, make sure you have everything with you."

Aunt Rosa gave him a look. "I may not like air travel but I'm not senile. Yet." She patted a capacious handbag. "I've got my passport, my boarding pass, my euros, and my sunglasses. And yes, my medication too, before you ask." She shook her head. "You remind me of your mother sometimes."

Harry got out of the car and opened the door for her, offering her his hand to help her out.

She beamed at him. "My sister said you were polite. Maybe you can teach *this* one a thing or two." She inclined her head toward Tony.

Harry gave her a polite smile. "I think Tony's manners are impeccable."

Tony jerked his head at that and his eyes lit up, but he said nothing. He got the carry-on suitcase from the boot, and with Aunt Rosa between them, they escorted her across the covered walkway and into the terminal, Tony pulling the case behind him.

Once inside, they went up the escalator to Departures, and paused at the entrance.

"You got all your liquids in a bag, ready?" Tony asked.

Aunt Rosa let out an exasperated sound. "Yes, for the second time." She reached up and curved her hand around his cheek. "Thank you for making the trip here so pleasant. It completely took my mind off the flight." She glanced at Harry. "For me, anticipation is the worst part of the journey. Once I'm here, I can relax a little."

Harry leaned over and kissed her cheek. "So when you're through Security, you can find a restaurant and sit down for a cup of tea or coffee."

Tony coughed, and Aunt Rosa's eyes gleamed. "Coffee? I'm heading for Wetherspoon's for a G&T." She snorted. "There have to be some perks to flying." She patted his arm. "It was lovely to meet you, Harry. I hope to see you again."

"Thanks, and likewise."

Aunt Rosa offered her cheek to Tony, but he enfolded her in a tight hug. "You look after yourself, you hear? And don't go chatting up too many Spanish men."

She rolled her eyes. "You're no fun." Aunt Rosa's gaze flickered toward Harry. "Don't lose this one."

"I have no intention of letting him get away," Tony said in a stage whisper, before glancing across at Harry.

His words filled Harry with warmth.

After yet more goodbyes, they stood and watched until Aunt Rosa had disappeared from view. Tony turned to Harry, smiling. "That's her taken care of, and it's only nine o'clock. Ready for what's next?"

"How can I be ready for it? I have no idea

what you're planning," Harry remonstrated.

Tony gestured toward the elevator. "Then it'll be a surprise. If you need a pee, I'd go now, because it'll be an hour at least before we get where we're going."

"Are you going to tell me at some point?"

Tony grinned. "When we get there."

Harry gave up. It was obviously much easier to go with the flow.

Speaking of flow…

The bathroom was a really good idea after all that coffee.

Tony spotted the signpost ahead and wondered if Harry had seen it. The idea for the visit had come to him as soon as he'd looked at the map. He'd seen the castle from a train once, its walls lit up by the afternoon sun, and he'd wondered what it was like inside.

The prospect of discovering it with Harry filled him with contentment.

"Arundel?" Harry looked across at him. "I've heard of it. Isn't there a medieval castle there?"

"Yup. And before you ask, no, I've never been there, but from the sound of it, neither have you, which I was actually hoping was the case. So now we get to see it together." He pointed as they turned a corner. "In fact, there it is." The castle rose up in front of them, clearly visible against the skyline above the town.

Harry's breathing hitched. "Oh wow. That

looks incredible. Like something out of a fairy story."

"Yeah, all we need now is a dragon, and a princess that needs rescuing." He leered. "Although, personally speaking? I'd prefer it to be a prince. You know, with those tights that show off everything?"

Harry snickered. "You have a one-track mind. Has anyone ever told you this?"

Tony guffawed. "They might have." He drove through the town, scanning the street signs. "There are a couple of car parks around here, just outside the castle walls. Once we get there, we can start with a drink in their coffee shop. Apparently, there's loads of things to see. Plus, there are gardens too. I thought we'd make a day of it." He glanced at Harry. "Does that sound all right?"

Harry let out a contented sigh. "I think it all sounds great. This is a wonderful idea."

Tony gave a shrug. "I thought it was better than going somewhere in London and ending up in a bar. It's a beautiful day, so let's enjoy it." Then he let out a triumphant noise. "There it is. Crown Yard car park." He turned into the entrance of the small parking area and peered intently, seeking a space.

"There's one." Harry pointed to an empty parking bay in the centre.

"Nicely spotted." The whole area only had about ten to fifteen spaces. "The guide book wasn't kidding when it said this place was tiny." Tony eased the Mini into the space, then switched off the engine. He reached into the glove box and removed a plastic bag full of coins. "Here's my change. I'll get stuff from the back if you go to the machine and get us a ticket. Put at least four hours on it? Maybe six?"

"Sure." Harry got out of the car. Tony got out too and went to the boot to remove the backpack. Mum had been busy in the kitchen that morning and had surprised him. Tony couldn't wait to see Harry's face when he opened the bag.

Tony leaned against the car, his gaze focused on Harry as he crossed the car park, a ticket in his hand. He knew so little about the man who had somehow got under his skin.

Maybe this is just what we need. A leisurely stroll through a gorgeous castle and its grounds, and a chance to learn more about each other.

Because based on what he'd seen thus far, Tony knew Harry was something special, and he was hoping Harry felt the attraction too.

Chapter Fifteen

"This place is gorgeous," Harry whispered as they strolled through the library.

Tony nodded absently, staring up at the vaulted wooden ceilings, the upper gallery, the red-and-cream carpet, the plush red velvet sofas that sat at intervals, and of course, the shelves upon shelves of books, safely secured behind metal lattice gates. The entire library glowed with the warm tones of the wood. "Imagine living here."

Harry chuckled. "Somehow I think my furniture might get a bit... lost in all this."

"Well, don't make any plans to move in just yet," Tony said with a snicker. "The family still live here." The Armoury and the Baron's Hall had been impressive, but the Regency library had to be the castle's crowning glory.

"I saw a poster as we came in. They have jousting here!"

Tony loved the way Harry's face lit up when he enthused about something. When his stomach gave a low growl, Tony coughed. "Sorry about that. I guess I'm hungry."

"Considering what time your day started, I'm not surprised." Harry cocked his head to one side. "There's a restaurant here, isn't there?"

"There is, but I've got a much better idea. How about a picnic lunch outside? We can find a spot with a good view, and then after, we'll go look at the gardens."

Harry peered at him intently. "And you just *happen* to have a picnic lunch on you, I suppose."

"Mum *might* have packed us a little something this morning." Tony held up his hands. "It wasn't my idea, honest. When I got up this morning, she'd been awake for hours. And when she gets like that, she cooks, she bakes, and pretty soon the fridge and freezer are full to bursting." He waggled his eyebrows. "You are gonna *die* when you taste my mum's tortilla."

"Tortilla? Isn't that a flat bread?"

Tony snickered. "Not in Spain. It's their word for omelette. You ever had Spanish omelette before?"

Harry frowned. "Omelette? For a picnic lunch?"

Tony chuckled. "Tortilla is made with two ingredients—potatoes and eggs. *Lots* of eggs. And it's delicious. You can have it hot or cold. We've got a box of Russian salad too, made the way Mum used to make it back in Malaga." He stilled. "Do you like green olives?"

"Yes. Any more surprises?"

"Garlic mayo to go with the tortilla, and of course, some of Mum's pastries for later." Another rumble from his stomach interrupted his flow, and Tony laughed. "Okay, no more talking. Let's eat, before we disturb the visitors with my noisy belly."

"I was gonna say—this *is* a library, after all." Harry's eyes gleamed with amusement.

Tony led the way toward the exterior, unable to stop smiling.

This was shaping up to be a great day.

Tony had to admit, the Collector Earl's Garden was a bit over-the-top for his tastes. A long pond was surrounded by tall pillars mounted by heavy-looking urns in the same warm-coloured stone. Still, it gave the garden a peaceful atmosphere.

They wandered through the differing gardens, admiring the fountains, the flowers, and the neatly cut box hedges. The trickle of water was a pleasant backdrop to the wealth of colours and fragrances that stirred their senses. Archways covered in foliage, surrounded a fountain where a chubby Eros clutched a fish, from whose mouth spewed a steady stream of water into the pond beneath.

Harry stopped by a stone bench between two terracotta troughs containing miniature palm trees. "Can we sit here for a bit?"

"Sure." Tony dumped the much lighter backpack onto the ground and sat beside him, taking in the flower beds and the chirping of birds that filled the air. For a moment, neither of them said a word, both sitting up straight, their faces turned toward the sun.

Harry closed his eyes, and Tony took advantage of the opportunity to look him up and down. Those jeans, the way they clung to his thighs, the T-shirt with its V-neck that hinted at the hair beneath it…

He has no idea what he does to me.

Just then a young couple strolled by, holding

hands and giggling. Now and again they paused to take pictures, the young woman posing for him, smiling. Then they'd walk on, oblivious to everyone else.

"God, how quickly life changes," Harry murmured, his gaze trained on them.

Something in Harry's voice stilled him. "What do you mean?"

Harry let out a heavy sigh. "One minute you're young and pretty—" Tony snickered, and Harry smacked him on the arm. "Hey. I was young and pretty once."

"Weren't we all?" Tony said with a chuckle. "Except you're not exactly a pensioner, mate. You're thirty-five."

"And when I was twenty, I was living in London, spending all my nights enjoying myself… and then everything changed. Dad passed, Mum got ill, and I quit my job to move in with her. That's how I came to be working at the recruitment office. It was near where she lived, so that meant less time away from her." He fell silent.

Tony said nothing. He had a feeling there was more to come, and as his grandma used to say, 'better out than in.' He didn't have long to wait.

Harry stared at him in silence, his expression grave. "I envy you, you know."

Tony blinked. "Me? Why?"

"You seem to really enjoy your life. You're always smiling, you always seem happy with your lot. *My* life just pisses me off."

"Mum says life is what you make it. So what's pissing you off about yours?"

Harry huffed. "I'm thirty-five and I'm still living in the house I grew up in. And it still looks exactly as it did then."

Tony gaped at him. "Wait a minute. *I'm* still at home too, remember? Sleeping in the same room I did when I was a kid. In my book, you have it way better. Christ, you're a homeowner."

"So what?"

Tony took a deep breath. "So what? So bleedin' *what*? I would love to have my own place. Why do you think I'm saving up every penny I get? So I can move out of the house where I can barely have a wank without hearing my mum downstairs, moaning or bitching about something, telling me to do this, do that…" He paused to take another breath. "I want a place that's mine. Not rented. Mine, so I can do whatever the hell I like with it." He shook his head. "I mean, yes, I love my family, but good grief—try living with a Spanish family when you're thirty. You've met Mum. Imagine living with that full time."

When Harry's eyes misted over, Tony's heart sank, and he cursed himself for being so blunt. He had no doubt it was the mention of his mum that had caused this reaction.

"Mum left me that house," Harry said quietly.

Tony stilled. "Really? Wow. I mean, it's sad that she died when she did, but she was obviously thinking about taking care of your future." Before he said something stupid about the cost of properties these days, he changed tack. "It must have been tough," he acknowledged. "Being with her when she was ill, then losing her." He might complain about Mum a lot, but the idea that one day she'd be gone forever? He didn't even want to contemplate *that* eventuality.

Harry swallowed. "I had to watch her die. Had to sit by while this bright, intelligent woman faded before my eyes. It was the hardest thing I've ever had to go through." He wiped his eyes. "Her death and everything that went before it sapped all my strength, my motivation, my passion for life."

Tony finally had a glimpse into what had shaped Harry's life, and all he wanted to do was hold him.

"Take the house, for instance. Every time I look at it, I cringe. It need so much doing to it, but I've no motivation to change it. My life is reduced to work, evenings in front of the TV, and those bloody weekend lists."

The glimmer of an idea sparked in Tony's head. "When you picture the house, what bugs you most?"

Harry's reaction was instantaneous. "That kitchen. White Formica doors, black plastic handles. It screams seventies."

Tony could deal with that. "But that's just cosmetic. That can be changed. And you know what? That's exactly what we're gonna do."

Harry gazed at him with such a perplexed expression that Tony had to laugh.

"You and me, we're gonna pay a visit to B&Q. We'll look at kitchens. Just *look*, all right? Just to get some ideas. Then we'll take it from there."

"You make it sound so easy."

Tony leaned in and whispered, "That's because it is. Trust me."

Harry pulled back and locked gazes with him. Tony was a sucker for sexy eyes, and Harry's were hazel, warm and inviting. "And that's the weird part. I've known you for what, three weeks? Yet it feels like much longer—and I do trust you."

Hearing those simple words sent a flood of calm through him. "I'm glad about that. And I know what you mean. It may only have been three weeks, but we've crammed a lot in." He covered Harry's hand with his own, loving the smooth feel of his skin beneath Tony's calloused fingers. "My day doesn't feel right until I've seen you walk by."

Harry chuckled. "And my day definitely feels better once I've got a glimpse of that builder's bum of yours, peeking above your Levis."

"I see. You been ogling my arse?" Tony grinned. He loved how the flecks of green in Harry's eyes seemed to become more vibrant when he was being cheeky, like tiny emeralds glinting in the sun.

"And the rest." Harry's eyes sparkled. "Well, if you *will* wear nothing but a pair of tight jeans…"

Arundel Castle may have been beautiful, but right then it was the last place Tony wanted to be. "You know I said we'd play by whatever rules made you feel comfortable?" Harry nodded. "So if I was to invite myself to your place tonight…" He left it there. Harry wasn't stupid.

Harry sat so still that for a moment, Tony thought he'd overstepped the mark again. Then he added almost nonchalantly, "I added a new item to my shopping list this week." There was something about that smile, the glint in his eyes, that hinted at…

Holy crap. Tony hoped to God Harry was saying what Tony *thought* he was saying… Forcing himself not to reveal just how much the prospect thrilled him, Tony merely nodded calmly. "Okay. Would I like this new item?"

"Oh, I think so. Maybe we should try one out tonight. Maybe a couple of them." He turned Tony's hand palm upward and ran his fingers over the thickened pads. "These are working hands, yet last week, they felt so soft." His gaze met Tony's, and memories of that shower came flooding back. His hand around Harry's shaft…

Tony's dick was definitely following the conversation with interest, and Tony struggled not to adjust it. Harry's gaze flickered downward, and then he laughed.

"How long will it take us to get back to Croydon?"

Arundel Castle had just lost its appeal.

Chapter Sixteen

By the time they reached Harry's place, it was almost six o'clock. During the almost two-hour trip, they'd listened to the radio, interrupting now and then with comments on the music. Harry found it amusing that both of them appeared keen to keep the conversation light. He was doing his damnedest not to think about what was coming up… in case something didn't. It had been *way* too long since he'd done this, but judging by the rock in his jeans, something *not* coming up wasn't going to be a problem. And the way Tony kept squirming in his seat?

Hard-ons could be bloody uncomfortable.

Tony switched off the engine and turned to regard Harry, his eyes bright. "Here we are then."

Harry smirked. "Is this where I invite you in for a coffee?"

A slow smile spread across Tony's face. "Skip the coffee. Let's go upstairs."

Harry's heartbeat sped up, and he swore he could feel the blood throbbing in his cock. "Want to take a shower first?"

Tony's smile widened. "Nah. I don't want you smelling of bodywash—I want to smell *you*. Now let's get out of this car, before my dick breaks my zip. These are my favourite jeans." He winked before opening the car door and climbing out. Harry followed him, his pulse growing more rapid. When they reached the front door, he fumbled as he removed his key from his pocket.

Tony laid a gentle hand on his. "No rushing, okay? Nice and easy."

Harry caught his breath. "It's not like I'm a virgin, right? I'm just a little… out of practice. And I've never brought a guy here for—"

"I get it. And as for being out of practice, it's like riding a bike." Tony's gaze flickered to Harry's crotch. "Only with a fair comfier saddle."

Harry managed to get indoors before all his neighbours could wonder why he was laughing like an idiot.

Once the door was locked, Harry hung up his jacket and waited as Tony removed his. "Do you want something to drink?" he asked as he removed his shoes and placed them on the shoe rack beneath the hall mirror.

"A glass of water would be nice." He did likewise, kicking off his boots.

Harry headed into the kitchen, grabbed two glasses from the cupboard, and stood facing the window as he waited for the water to run cooler: it had been a hot day. He gave a little start when Tony slipped his arms around his waist, before kissing his neck. Strong hands stroked his belly, while Tony nuzzled him, sucking at the skin. A shiver coursed through him, and Tony chuckled against his neck. "You like this."

Harry stifled a moan. "What gave me away?" He shuddered when Tony reached higher to brush his fingers over the nipples that pushed against the cotton of his T-Shirt. "You can't do that *and* expect me to fill two glasses at the same time. Way too distracting."

Tony paused his hands. "Go on. I'll play nice. But it's not *my* fault if I can't stop touching you."

"I suppose it's mine," Harry said as he turned off the tap and placed the glasses on the work surface next to the sink. Tony's remark about a comfier saddle had him wondering, and he guessed there was no time like the present. "Can I ask… if we're talking about riding…"

Tony's lips brushed against his ear. "You wanna know who's ridin' who?" His breath tickled.

"Unless it's a secret," Harry quipped.

"Well, now that you mention it…" Strong hands grasped Harry's shoulders, turning him around to face Tony. He moved a hand lower, until he was cupping Harry's erection. "Want this inside me. Does that work for you?" His eyes glittered.

Harry figured saying *Fuck yeah* was a little over the top. "Definitely." His voice sounded gruff.

Tony's eyes shone. "Then what are we waiting for?" He picked up the glasses. "Bedroom," he said in a low, firm voice. "And yes, too right it's your fault if I can't stop touching you. You shouldn't be so fucking sexy. Now get up them stairs so I can undress you, slowly."

Harry walked out of the kitchen, Tony close behind him, and hurried toward the staircase. He heard the creak of the treads as Tony followed, and the first thing he did on entering his bedroom was to dash across the room and hastily draw the curtains across the bay window.

Tony laughed. "Good thinking. You don't want all your neighbours across the street peering in and watching. Mind you, it wouldn't be the first time I've had an audience."

Harry stared at him. "Seriously?"

Tony shrugged. "What can I say? It was a party, I was twenty-two, and I was pissed as a fart." He placed the glasses on the bedside cabinet, then beckoned Harry with a crooked finger. "Now come 'ere, sexy."

Harry crossed the bedroom floor to where Tony stood. "Look who's talking," he said softly.

Tony beamed. "You think I'm sexy, do ya?"

Harry said nothing, but ran his hands over Tony's muscled upper arms, sliding his fingers under the hem of his sleeves, the fabric stretched around his biceps. His heart pounding, he shifted a little closer and moved his hands higher to cup Tony's nape. Harry leaned in and kissed him, light and chaste, drinking in the scent that clung to his skin, his clothing, a warm, sensual aroma that only served to heighten his desire.

Tony responded, taking Harry in his arms, stroking his back, his shoulders, then moving lower to tug Harry's T-shirt free of his jeans. "Tops off," he said in a low voice. "Nothing else for now."

Harry was all for that. He helped Tony to remove the shirt, before repeating the action with Tony's shirt. Tony tossed the garments onto the carpet, then piled up the pillows, gesturing for Harry to lie down. He lay beside him, hooking his left thigh over Harry's right, and brought their mouths together in a leisurely kiss.

This was heaven. No haste, just unhurried kisses while they touched each other, fingers lightly caressing bare chests, exploring, discovering… Harry laid his hand on Tony's thigh as Tony stroked his belly, edging lower and lower until he encountered the waistband of Harry's jeans. Tony pulled back a little and looked him in the eye as he freed the button, then casually lowered the zip. He paused, as if awaiting instructions.

"Yes," Harry whispered.

There was that beaming smile again, and Tony's lips parted as he slid his fingers under Harry's briefs. Then all hesitancy vanished when he wrapped his hand around Harry's dick, rubbing it firmly.

"You've got a great dick, y'know." Tony alternated between fast and slow, until Harry was on the verge of begging him to *take it out, for God's sake.* When Tony shifted position, Harry sent up silent thanks and prepared to feel that hot mouth on his cock once more, but to his surprise, Tony removed his hand and instead, leaned over to kiss his shaft through the cotton that clung to it. Harry pushed up with his hips, wanting more, and Tony's gaze met his.

"I think these jeans need to come off too."

Harry lost no time in pushing off the offending article, Tony aiding him by tugging at the legs, but leaving his briefs in place. Harry took one look at his white socks and removed them too. Tony leaned over and kissed him.

"My turn," he said as he unfastened his own jeans and shoved them down and off. Harry couldn't miss the way Tony's cock poked out from beneath the briefs. Tony snickered. "It's trying to escape."

"Then let me help it." Harry reached into Tony's briefs and stroked his shaft and balls, Tony giving him greater access by pushing the fabric lower. He kissed Harry's shoulder as Harry slid his hand up and down his dick, closing his eyes and making small noises of contentment when Harry gently squeezed his balls. One look at Tony's parted lips was all the invitation Harry needed.

He shifted onto his side, his hand still gripping Tony's thick cock, and leaned closer to kiss him, sighing with pleasure when Tony reached over to stroke his dick through his briefs. Another wave of kisses followed, only this time Harry claimed Tony's mouth, stroking his tongue between his lips, loving the way Tony moved on the bed, as if he was unable to keep still. Harry held the head of Tony's cock lightly between his thumb and a couple of fingers, keeping the movement quick as he played with it. Shudders rippled through Tony's body, and when Harry curled his hand around the shaft to move it faster, he hurriedly drew his knees higher and removed his briefs.

"Where are your condoms and lube? In the drawer?"

Harry pointed to the bedside cabinet beside them. "In there."

Tony moved to straddle Harry, one hand on his shoulder, the other clutching the headboard while he bent over to kiss him. Their lips joined as Tony rocked slowly back and forth, and Harry could feel the heat of him through his briefs. The motion was leisurely, a gentle undulation, Harry's dick rubbing through Tony's crease. Harry gazed up at him, admiring the way his abs flexed as he moved, his strong thighs, the drag of his heavy cock against Harry's belly. Harry stroked Tony's waist and the small of his back, before moving lower to slide a finger between his arse cheeks.

Tony shivered. "Yeah." He rocked a little faster, his cock pushing through the circle of Harry's hand as he leaned back on his hands, his hips rolling.

"Oh, yeah, that dick is gonna feel so good inside me."

Harry wanted more than Tony's dick in his hand.

He wanted Tony's cock in his mouth.

"Up here," he instructed, grabbing Tony around the waist and tugging him higher up the bed. Tony knelt up on one knee, held his shaft steady as he rubbed the head over Harry's lips, then filled his mouth with hard bare flesh.

Fuck, the taste of him…

"God, that feels amazing." Tony held onto the headboard and thrust, his need visibly increasing as Harry hastily removed his own briefs, not pausing once in his enjoyment of Tony's cock. He sucked hard on the head, loving the shudders that multiplied throughout Tony's body with each fresh new sensual assault. Tony stretched over to pull open the drawer, and then dropped a condom and the lube onto the bed beside them. "Get me ready."

Harry wasted no time. He slicked up his fingers, then sought Tony's hot little hole, sliding them into him while he continued to take his dick deep. Tony rocked between his mouth and his fingers, before reaching behind him to grab Harry's cock and slap it against his pucker.

Harry gasped around his mouthful of hot dick, and pulled free of it. He drew Tony down to him in a breathless kiss, his hands caressing Tony's nape and back, and Tony rocked against his erect dick. "Ready?" Harry asked him, tilting his hips to slide his shaft through Tony's crack. Tony grabbed the condom packet and thrust it into Harry's hands. Harry snickered. "I'll take that as a yes."

He tore it open and gloved up, his dick

aching. Tony positioned himself above it, the head softly kissing his hole, and Harry resisted the urge to drive his shaft deep into that welcome heat. Instead, he held his cock steady as Tony sank down onto it, until every last inch of his dick was buried inside Tony's tight body.

"Oh my fucking God, you're long." Tony shivered. "Gimme a sec, all right?"

Fucking bliss. To Harry's mind, the only thing that beat the sensation of having a hot body wrapped around his cock was the equally glorious moment when a hard dick entered him. There was little to choose from between the two.

"Okay, that's better." Tony bent over and took his lips in a fevered kiss. "Now fuck me."

Harry lost himself in Tony's heat while they kissed, Harry's hands spreading Tony's arse as he moved in and out of him, picking up a little speed.

"Fuck, you feel good inside me." Tony's words trailed off into a moan when Harry gave an extra hard thrust. "God, yeah, that's it. Go as hard as you like."

He wrapped his arms around Tony's waist and held him tightly, fucking him with longer strokes. Tony nodded energetically, his hands gripping Harry's waist. "Just like that. You're pegging it. Don't stop, for fuck's sake, don't stop." Noises continued to poured from him, a soft litany of 'yeah' and 'fuck' and 'oh', and he deepened their kisses, his tongue eagerly seeking Harry's. When Tony broke a kiss to beg him, "Flip me over", Harry held onto him and did just that, his dick slipping out of Tony as they rolled over, then Tony rolled again to lie on his front, spreading his legs wide and presenting himself, arse tilted.

"Come on, fill me."

Harry aimed for that pink, glistening hole and speared Tony with his cock, sliding all the way into him until he was balls deep. Tony's loud groan of pleasure reverberated around the room, and Harry withdrew, only to slide in faster and harder, his hands anchored on Tony's waist.

"Oh yeah, that's right. Fucking *perfect*." Tony pushed back, fucking himself on Harry's dick, and Harry watched the rippling muscles across his back as he moved. Tony being fucked was a thing of beauty. When he stilled, Harry paused too, his cock wedged inside him.

"Want to see you," Tony gasped out.

Harry pulled free, and Tony flipped onto his back, drawing his knees up to his chest. Harry grabbed hold of Tony's thighs, guided his cock into position, and filled Tony to the hilt. Tony let go of his legs and pulled Harry closer, until Harry was lying between his thighs, hips rolling as he fucked Tony with faster and faster strokes, his arms hooked under Tony's knees.

Tony ran his hands over Harry's belly and chest. "Fuckin' beautiful bear," he growled. He tweaked Harry's nipples, and Harry felt the first tingle of electricity, the herald of his orgasm. "Look at you, all this fucking gorgeous hair, this firm belly. Just seeing you like this makes me wanna come." Tony tugged on his cock, his hand a blur, while he stroked and caressed Harry's body. He arched his back, his mouth open, and that was all the warning Harry got before warm come hit him in the middle of his chest. Tony shuddered beneath him, tiny spurts of spunk still pulsing from his dick, his chest flushed a deep red.

The sight of Tony climaxing was all it took to have Harry shooting his load, his shaft locked inside Tony, throbbing as he filled the latex. He cupped Tony's head in his hands and kissed him fervently, the two of them clinging to each other, their bodies slick with sweat.

Little by little, the last jolts ebbed away, until they lay on the bed, Harry trying his hardest not to squash Tony with his body. Tony shifted, pulling him down onto the bed, then wrapped his arms around him, fusing their lips in yet more kisses.

Tony let out a tired sigh. "God, I'd forgotten how good sex wipes you out."

Harry cackled. "Let's be honest here. *Any* sex wipes you out, if it's strenuous enough."

"Maybe, but that was definitely good sex."

Harry decided the time for holding back was long gone. "Do you top too?"

Tony's smile was answer enough. *Thank God for that.*

Chapter Seventeen

Tony stretched beneath the single sheet. It had been a warm night, but not so warm that he'd wanted to relinquish his hold on Harry. Tony had slept curled around him, breathing him in.

I could get used to sharing a bed.

Not that there had been a great number of applicants for that position. Sure, there had been a few guys in the past ten years, but none of them had lasted more than a couple of months. The break-ups had felt… organic, none of them acrimonious or unpleasant: the relationships had simply run their natural course.

So why am I hoping that this one will last?

Granted, it was early days. Three weeks was a mere blip on anyone's radar, but Tony couldn't shake the feeling that Harry could be more than a flash in the pan.

I want this to work.

Yet despite their conversation in the gardens the previous day, Tony knew there was so much that he didn't know about Harry, including the biggest mystery of all—why he was so down on himself.

I could always ask him.

Tony smiled to himself. How did that line go from the cartoons he watched as a kid? It was so crazy that it just might work. He knew what had pulled him to Harry initially had been Harry's appearance, but since then there had been glimpses of the man Harry kept hidden. Glimpses which had only served to confuse Tony even more. Here was a man who was clearly a good boss, judging by the way he'd handled Simon, and yet he appeared to have so few friends. *Does he have any?* Harry's reaction to the abandoned kitten was another case in point. Tony's heart had melted at the sight of Harry gently holding the kitten, his genuine concern for the cute little girl.

Harry was definitely a conundrum. He seemed to be a man with a fondness for people and animals, yet appeared to be filled with what Tony could only describe as self-loathing.

What makes you tick, Harry? What is it about you that pulls me in and keeps me here?

Harry stirred beside him, then slowly rolled over to face him. "Morning," he said sleepily. "Wha' time is it?"

"Too early to get up on a Sunday," Tony said, stroking Harry's beard. "A perfect morning for lying in bed as long as we want, doing whatever we want." He knew what *he* wanted—Harry's question the previous night about topping had left him in no doubt whatsoever about *that*—but Tony wasn't about to initiate anything. He'd learned his lesson.

Harry gave him a drowsy smile that was utterly adorable. "Does this perfect morning include coffee?"

Tony laughed. "Yeah, very subtle." He leaned over and kissed Harry's cheek. "I'll be back," he said in his best Arnie voice.

Harry snickered.

Tony climbed out of bed, briefly considered putting on his underwear, then decided against it. Anyone who could see his tackle through Harry's net curtains had to be armed with a high-powered telescope, and if that was how they got their jollies, more power to them. He padded down the stairs and into the kitchen. The floral blind was drawn, casting a warm glow about the room. Tony put the kettle on, then went to the cabinet where he knew Harry kept his coffee. When he opened it and saw a brand-spanking new cafetière sitting there, along with a bag of medium roast ground coffee, he had to smile.

You sneaky little devil. It warmed him that Harry had followed his advice.

Tony peered into the fridge, seeking ingredients for breakfast. What disturbed him was how little food it contained. *What does he eat?* It didn't matter. Tony could find them a nice place for breakfast, or brunch. Still, this wasn't the first time he'd noticed the lack of food.

Tony pushed aside his unease and set about making coffee.

Ten minutes later, he'd found a tray, and ladened it with the cafetière now full of brewing coffee, two mugs, a sugar bowl, and a small jug of milk. Still smiling, he carried it carefully upstairs to Harry's bedroom. On impulse, he paused at the door of the rear bedroom, which was ajar. It was filled with boxes, piled up on the floor and the bed.

Tony wondered if it had been Harry's room as a child.

He entered the bedroom and set the tray down at the foot of the bed. "Someone's been shopping."

Harry cleared his throat. "It's very... disconcerting having you walking naked around the house."

Tony raised his eyebrows. "Are you

complaining? Want me to put something on?" He straightened, knowing full well his dick was already at half-mast and pointing right at Harry.

"You could put someone's eye out with that," Harry said with a snicker.

Tony snorted. "That doesn't answer my question. Are you complaining?" He swung his cock from side to side, and it landed against his hips with a resounding slap. When Harry laughed, Tony came around to Harry's side and stood close to the bed. "Better watch your eyes," he said, smirking.

And then all thoughts of coffee fled when Harry opened for him.

The coffee wasn't about to go cold, because the way Harry sucked dick? Tony would be shooting his load down Harry's throat before you could say Pass the sugar. Sure enough, before the steam had finally dissipated, Tony was shuddering as he bent over, clutching the headboard while Harry drank down every last drop of come.

"I think you might just have set a record," Tony gasped, shivering as Harry cleaned his cock with a warm tongue. Harry gazed up at him with an inquiring glance, and the combination of a hot, wet mouth around the head of his dick and those hazel eyes locked on his was enough to give Tony second thoughts about his plans for their Sunday.

Harry slowly released his cock and gazed at him inquiringly. "Oh?"

"Don't think I've ever come so fast in my life."

Harry gestured to the empty spot beside him. "Get in, while I pour us some coffee. Who knows, I might try to beat that record later."

Tony liked this new Harry, not for his

obvious delight in sucking cock, but because he exuded a new confidence that was very attractive.

Yeah, Tony wasn't about to lose this one. And as for his plans, well, they could wait a while.

Some things were more important.

Harry gaped at the price list sitting on the glossy black marble kitchen worktop. "*How* much?" They'd spent the last twenty minutes walking through B&Q's display of kitchens, and he was beginning to regret the whole idea. Eight grand for a kitchen? Okay, so some of them looked great, but still… Eight grand?

Tony snickered. "Okay, remember I said we're here to look, right? This trip is just to work out what you like." He pointed to the price list. "And that's the price for buying and installing the kitchen. We don't pay any attention to that."

"We don't?"

Tony shook his head. "For a start, that includes all the base units. You don't need them. I know, 'cause I checked them out this morning. You just need new doors. What you *don't* have are enough wall cabinets, and that floral countertop has got to go."

Harry couldn't have agreed more. "So, what are we doing here?"

Tony had to smile. "You're talking to a builder, remember? You just need to show me which ones you like, then leave it to me. I'll buy whatever you need at cost from a building supply company.

And as for paying someone to fit it…." He grinned
and flexed his arms, his muscles bulging. "You got
me. Not that I'll be working alone. I've already got
someone in mind to be my builder's mate."

"Who?" Harry hadn't considered that
prospect, but it stood to reason that Tony couldn't do
it all himself.

Tony's grin didn't falter. "You."

Harry blinked. "Me? I'd be about as much
use as a chocolate teapot." He wasn't a practical man
by any means. Heaven forbid a fuse should blow:
he'd be useless.

"You can make tea and coffee, right? Hand
me a hammer and nails? Hold the step ladder steady?
Shit like that?" Tony placed a gentle hand on his
arm. "Don't worry, it won't be that difficult a task.
The wall units are a piece of piss to assemble, and
hanging the doors is easy-peasy. The only tricky bit
is cutting the work top to fit right. Thank God it's all
straight pieces in your kitchen." He gestured to the
displays. "So? Which one lights your candle? If I
have an idea of what you're after, I can find a couple
of possibles. Then I'll just send you photos and you
can choose." Tony stroked the black marble surface.
"This, for instance. Do you like the idea of black?
Stone? Granite? Or something warmer, like oak or
beech?"

Harry groaned. "Slow down. Too many
choices!"

Tony laughed. "Okay. Let's do this a step at
a time."

As they examined the displays, Harry found
himself growing more excited. Finally, a step in the
right direction. He couldn't picture the kitchen the
way Tony obviously could, but he trusted Tony's

judgment.

As for Tony, Harry was starting to think that agreeing to go for a drink with him three weeks ago was probably the smartest thing he'd ever done. He had to admit Tony was good for him. After all, it was having Tony around that had pushed Harry into tackling his weight issues, albeit with small steps. Although he was beginning to think maybe he was overdoing it a little. The hardest part was hiding his present eating habits from Tony.

Not for much longer. Just until I can drop a size in my jeans and shirts become less tight around my belly. So what if Tony thought Harry was a bear—surely there was such a thing as an overweight bear?

Chapter Eighteen

Tony swiped through the photos on his phone. He had a better idea of what Harry wanted, and was confident he could find the perfect kitchen range. So what if he'd spend the following weekend getting all hot and sweaty in a small space?

There were other ways to get hot and sweaty with Harry that were far more fun. And speaking of Harry... Tony walked into the kitchen where Harry was rustling up some food for their dinner.

"What are we having?"

"Corned beef and salad," Harry said without turning his head. "That okay?"

It was on the tip of Tony's tongue to ask if that would be enough for them, seeing as they hadn't eaten lunch but had had a large breakfast. Well, *Tony* had—Harry had picked at his, and claimed he wasn't all that hungry. *How can anyone not be hungry for breakfast?* Tony was ravenous most mornings, but especially after sex.

"Sounds good." He walked over to Harry and put his arms around him. Tony buried his face in Harry's neck. Fuck, he smelled good. The feel of that firm body in his arms and Harry's scent stirred his senses. Harry stilled and turned his head slightly, his lips parted, and Tony was suddenly aware of those green flecks in his hazel eyes. *So sexy...*

Harry cleared his throat. "Dinner won't exactly go cold, will it?" His voice was husky.

Tony leaned in and nuzzled his neck. "Got

something better in mind than dinner?" He kissed Harry's earlobe, before gently pulling on it with his teeth. Harry's shiver was delicious. Tony brushed his lips over the shell of Harry's ear. "Put the plates in the fridge, Harry. Because… warm, limp salad? Ew." On impulse he shifted his hand lower to below the push of Harry's belly where his fingers met a stony ridge in Harry's jeans. "Nothing limp here." Tony casually reached around to give Harry's arse a gentle squeeze. He sought the rigid back seam and rubbed it firmly, loving the low moan that tumbled from Harry's lips, as though he'd been unable to prevent its escape.

"Yes," Harry whispered, and Tony was under no illusions as to what he meant.

"Where?" Tony demanded, his voice as husky as Harry's had been. "Couch? Bed?"

"Upstairs."

That was all it took to galvanize Tony into action. He grabbed the plates and went to the fridge. Harry moved fast and opened it for him. Their dinner safely stowed, Harry seized Tony's hand and pulled him out of the kitchen, along the hallway and up the stairs. No words passed between them, and that was fine by Tony. There'd be plenty of time for talking later.

Right then, dirty talking was pretty high on his list of preferred activities, along with getting his first taste of Harry's hole.

This was not going to be like their first time. Harry didn't want slow and steady. He ached to be fucked, to feel Tony's length filling him, stretching him. As sweet as Tony's arse had been, Harry couldn't wait to feel that meaty dick inside him.

Then he reasoned that maybe slow and steady was better. It had been a while, after all.

Tony inclined his head toward the curtains. "Shall I close them?" he inquired, his eyes twinkling.

Harry laughed. "Like you have to ask." Anticipation thrummed through him, leaving him tingling. There was enough sunlight filtering through the curtains that they didn't need a light on, which was fine by Harry. Right then he didn't want to see—he wanted to *feel.*

Tony got onto the bed and opened his arms wide. "Come 'ere, you."

Harry climbed onto the bed and lay beside him. "Bossy." He liked that Tony didn't start stripping off immediately. God knew, in his twenties Harry had experienced his fair share of hook-ups where the only goal had been to insert tab A into slot B in as fast a time as possible. Sure, he'd gotten off, but that was then. His first time with Tony had brought with it an appreciation for taking time to *enjoy* him.

Their arms wound around each other, they kissed, Tony's previous urgency fading as he stroked Harry's beard. His touch was gentle, and Harry found the caress almost hypnotic. He invested himself fully in the kiss, breathing in Tony's cologne, the musky scent that was all him. Tony inserted his leg between Harry's, deepening their connection, and suddenly they were moving together, an unhurried, sensuous undulation. Harry cradled the back of Tony's head with one hand, while he stroked up and down his back, and the swell of his arse with the other.

Tony's hands were all over him, his shoulders, his neck, his chest, constantly moving, like he was learning the feel of Harry's body all over again. "Fuck, you can kiss," he murmured against Harry's lips. He grabbed Harry's hand and dragged it to his crotch, moulding it against his erection. "Feel what you do to me."

Harry cupped the hard outline, tracing it with his fingertips. "I really need you to fuck me right now."

Tony's breathing caught. "God, just the thought of sliding into you sends shivers through me." He shifted out of Harry's grasp, sat up, and pulled his shirt up and over his head.

Harry didn't waste a second. He copied Tony, hastily unbuttoning his shirt, slipping it off and tossing it aside. Then Tony hooked his jeans-encased leg over Harry's thigh, and it was right back to kissing, while Tony fumbled to open his jeans, revealing black briefs that did little to hide his hard shaft.

"Naked, now," Harry said, his voice a little raw. He undid his jeans and shoved them past his hips, and Tony quickly got rid of his own, kicking them off the bed onto the floor. Then they were in each other's arms, kissing like it was going out of fashion, both reaching for one another's dicks, stroking them together, Tony's thigh between Harry's.

"Can't stop touching you," Tony said between kisses. "Love this hair, the way it covers almost all of you." He snaked his hands up Harry's back. "Except here. Love that you're smooth here."

"And if I had a hairy back?" Harry inquired, grinning. "Would that be a deal breaker?"

Tony snorted. "We wouldn't be fucking at all. Hairy backs… ugh… makes me think of werewolf movies."

That was an image Harry didn't want in his head right then.

Then Tony laughed. "Sorry. I was kidding about the deal breaker bit. Besides, there's always Veet."

Harry almost choked with laughter.

Tony reached lower and grabbed a handful of arse cheek. "And this is nice. Smooth, round cheeks, but with a furry crease. Perfect. I fucking love a hairy crack."

Harry chuckled against his neck. "That's lucky." He gently pushed Tony onto his back, and leisurely laid a trail of kisses down over his chest and belly, until his lips met the head of Tony's cock.

"Fuck, yeah." Tony spread his legs wide, and Harry took him deep, all the while tugging on his own heavy dick. Tony cupped his balls and pushed deeper, one hand stroking Harry's back and shoulders while he made tiny thrusts with his hips, apparently unable to keep still. He moaned when Harry flicked the head with his tongue, and then expelled a long breath when Harry sucked hard on it, bringing his hand to hold the shaft steady. "God, Harry…."

Harry pulled free and took Tony once more into his arms, kissing him more passionately now, their hands moving over each other's bodies as they writhed on the bed, Harry lying between Tony's thighs, the heat between them increasing. Harry couldn't get enough of the feel of Tony's body beneath his fingers, the smooth, warm skin on his back, the pebbled flesh on his arse where a carpet of goose bumps had erupted, the soft hair on his thighs. But that mouth, those lips…

Tony's kisses were fucking addictive.

"Kneel up," Tony gasped out, breaking away for a moment. "Wanna suck your dick."

Harry scrambled to his knees, his hand on Tony's nape as Tony bobbed his head, his fingers circling the root of Harry's cock. Harry reached down to pull on Tony's dick, sliding up and down the warm shaft, revelling in its heat and girth.

In his hand was good. In his mouth was even better.

"Me too." Harry lay down on his side, his arm beneath Tony's thigh, Tony's thick cock right where he wanted it. He licked his lips, then wrapped his hand around the solid warm flesh and took him deep.

Tony's only reaction was to groan around Harry's dick, before sucking him even harder.

Fuck, it was heaven, sucking and licking, both feeding each other small noises of appreciation. Nothing hurried, only the slow enjoyment of Tony's dick, savouring the taste of him, the feel of satin-soft skin, the stickiness of precome on his lips.

Tony broke off his obviously pleasurable experience, and gasped out, "Fuck. Love your cock."

Harry took a breath. "Then don't stop," he ground out.

The next moment, Harry groaned out loud when a slick finger circled his hole, while Tony renewed his savouring of Harry's dick. Harry bent his leg and gently rocked his hips, wanting more, and Tony obliged, softly probing his tight pucker.

God, how could he concentrate on the task in hand when Tony was sucking and fingering him to perfection? He slid an arm under Tony's thigh and took a firm hold of Tony's shaft, holding it steady while he sucked on the wide head, both of them letting noises of sheer pleasure escape into the room.

Then Tony pulled free of Harry's body. "Get back up 'ere," he said quietly after pausing for a moment.

Harry shifted position until he was half lying on Tony, exploring him with his tongue, unable to refrain from kissing him. Fuck, if kissing were an Olympic event, Tony would have been a gold medallist.

"Still want me inside you?"

Harry let out a low moan of desire. "Yes." Tony wrapped his arms around him, then gently rolled him onto his back, before moving to lie between Harry's thighs. He stared down at Harry, arms locked at the elbow. "Fuck, look at you. All laid out for me."

"Has anyone ever told you that you talk too much?" Harry exclaimed.

Tony laughed. "Aww. You got something else in mind?" He kissed Harry's nipples, flicking them in turn with his tongue, and each time it sent a tingle racing down Harry's spine, straight to his dick. Tony raised his head, that grin still present. "Maybe something like that?"

"If you're gonna use your mouth, for fuck's sake, put it to good use!" Harry *wanted*.

Tony kissed his way lower, reaching Harry's cock, and Harry held his breath, awaiting that hot mouth around his length. When that didn't materialize, Harry came close to losing it.

Tony, it seemed, had another destination in mind—and a whole new activity.

He got off the bed, grabbed hold of Harry's hips and tugged him toward the foot of the bed, before kneeling there. Tony spread Harry's legs wide, pushing them higher, then bent over to casually lick a wet trail over his hole.

"Oh God," Harry groaned, grabbing his knees and pulling them toward his chest.

Tony's breath tickled his sac. "Been thinking about doing this all day." He got comfortable, leaning against the mattress, while he spread Harry's cheeks.

That first contact when Tony's warm, wet tongue pressed against his hole was like electricity shooting through him. Harry pushed his head back into the mattress, closed his eyes, and gave himself up to Tony's glorious sensual assault. Tony paused to kiss his arse cheeks, and Harry made a harsh sound at the back of his throat, before strangling out the words, "Fucking tease."

Tony's breath was hot against his hole, and suddenly Harry's throat tightened as Tony recommenced his tongue-fucking. His shivers multiplied, until he was quivering uncontrollably, his need to feel Tony's dick inside him white-hot.

"Come on, fuck me," he ground out, yet he lifted his shoulders up off the bed to grab Tony's head and hold him there, wanting more. Tony speared him with his tongue, and Harry cried out with sheer joy. "Again!"

Tony raised his head and laughed. "Well, make your mind up. Do you want me to fuck you with my tongue or my cock?" Harry growled at him, and Tony's laugh echoed around the bedroom. "Ooh, is that a tough decision?"

Harry was about to growl at him some more, but Tony stopped him with a slow press of his tongue into his hole, his breath hot against Harry's arse. "Oh my fucking God." Rimming had *never* been this good. Maybe he had Tony's Olympic skills all wrong. He dropped back onto the bed, reached down and pulled his cheeks apart, stretching his hole.

Tony apparently got the message, and soon Harry was shuddering as wave upon wave of bliss filled him, flooding through him until he couldn't take another second of Tony's talented tongue. "Fuck me," he pleaded.

Tony stopped what he was doing, got up from his kneeling position, and went around the bed to the cabinet that contained the condoms and lube. Harry held out his fingers for some of the slick liquid, and slid a couple of fingers into his own hole while he watched Tony covering his cock, which poked up, rigid, thick and dark. Tony pressed the slippery head against his body, and Harry held his breath, waiting for that delicious sensation of being penetrated.

Tony held his gaze, deliberately rubbing the head over Harry's hole, not applying any pressure. Harry squirmed, bearing down, desperate to feel that heat inside him.

Tony bit his lip. "Not gonna rush this. It's the best part." He shifted a little, and Harry breathed deeply as Tony eased the head past the tight muscle. Tony stilled, closing his eyes for a moment. "Oh fuck. Yeah. Best fucking feeling ever."

Harry wasn't going to disagree. He relished the burn, the blissful sensation of being stretched by a fat dick. Just when he was about to beg for more, Tony leisurely pushed inside him, and Harry shivered with each heady inch, until at last Tony was fully seated.

"Oh, fuck, you feel good." Tony leaned over to kiss him, and Harry held onto him as Tony gave a gentle roll of his hips, letting him grow accustomed to the feel of his dick. Harry stroked his cock, kissing Tony deeply as he moved in and out of him, Tony's hands all over him, on his chest, his belly, his thighs, never breaking the connection between them.

Then Tony adjusted his stance, spreading his legs, and grabbing onto Harry's thighs, he proceeded to slide a little faster, easing out of him unhurriedly, before thrusting harder to rob him of his breath. "Like that?"

Harry rolled his eyes. "Don't talk, fuck," he said, his voice raw. The exquisite sensation of Tony's dick stroking in and out of him, the thrusts that now had real power behind them, making him ache, making him sweat….

"What, like this?" Tony pumped into him, hips snapping, his hands holding tight onto Harry's thighs. Harry cried out, tugging harder on his cock, aware of each time Tony nudged his prostate, propelling him closer and closer to the edge.

"Oh, fuck, yeah," Harry groaned. "Just like that." But as good as it felt, there was something missing. "Tony? Hold me?"

Tony paused, slowly withdrawing his dick. "Shift up the bed. I'm gonna lie behind ya." Harry did as instructed, but when he tried to lie on his side, Tony stopped him. "Bring your leg up. Let me in."

It seemed like mere seconds before Tony was back inside him, his hand on Harry's hip as he rocked into him, Harry's arm beneath Tony's neck as they moved together. Tony kissed him, and Harry lost himself in the sensual motion of their bodies, his cock hard against his thigh.

It wouldn't be long.

"Want you to ride me," Tony gasped. "Wanna watch you when you come. Wanna feel it all over me. Feel you tight around my cock." Harry opened his mouth to protest, but Tony stopped his words with a fervent kiss. "And before you say a word, you're not gonna crush me, all right? You're not as heavy as you think you are. I want to see into your eyes when I make you come."

The heat in Tony's expression overrode Harry's fears. He straddled Tony, reaching back to ease his dick into him again, and Tony groaned. "God, yeah. That feels bloody good."

Harry wanted to move slowly, to make it last, but he was too far gone for that. He rocked back and forth, pulling on his cock, while Tony caressed his torso, lingering on his chest and belly. Harry trembled as his orgasm approached, and Tony exulted in his reaction, his gaze locked on Harry. "That's it, babe. Fucking come on me."

Then Tony reached up and squeezed Harry's nipples, before flicking them with the tips of his fingers.

Game Over.

Harry moaned as he shot his creamy load onto Tony's chest, and Tony's cries mingled with his. Tony pulled Harry down onto him, cupping his head while they kissed, Harry unable to stay still, shuddering through each mini jolt of ecstasy that ricocheted through his body. Tony tilted his hips and fucked up into him, his breath quickening, his body stiffening. Harry closed his eyes when he felt the throb of Tony's dick inside him, deepening their kiss, until Tony too lay quiet beneath him.

Harry carefully lifted himself off Tony's cock, and stretched out beside him, damp with sweat, and with a beautiful ache inside him. "God, I'd forgotten how good that feels."

Tony rolled onto his side, his still half-hard cock encased in latex, and ran his fingers over Harry's chest. "Okay, where have you been all my life? You fuck like a machine, and you have a hole made for fucking."

Harry snickered. "So what does that make me? Your dream guy?"

Tony stilled. "Pretty much, yeah."

What? Harry was shocked into inaction.

Tony put his weight on one elbow and stared at Harry. "Because there's more to you than looks and sex. The way you think. Your kind heart. Your emotions. Your strength. Your vulnerability."

Harry didn't know how to react. His face warmed. "Sure you're talking about me?" he joked. He'd never heard Tony speak in such a serious tone of voice, and somehow it added weight to his words.

Tony leaned over and kissed him softly on the lips. "Absofuckinglutely." His stomach growled, and Tony rolled his eyes. "Yeah, and that's dead romantic, right?"

Harry laughed, grateful for the interruption. "Dinner's in the fridge. How about we grab a quick shower first?" Tony's eyes lit up, and Harry waved a warning finger. "And no, you are *not* getting in with me. At this rate, we'd be eating at midnight."

Tony pouted. "Spoilsport." He carefully removed the condom, then got up off the bed. "Well, let me dump this in the bin, then you can have the first shower. Seeing as I'm a gentleman." When Harry arched his eyebrows, Tony snickered. "I am. I let you come first."

"*Let* me?" Harry gave him an expression of mock outrage, but inside he was laughing.

Tony was everything he'd ever wanted—but had never once dreamed he'd have.

Chapter Nineteen

Harry finished his last mouthful of coffee and glanced at the clock. For some reason, Wednesday was really dragging. Tony had texted him photos of the cabinet doors he'd found, and Harry had been delighted. His kitchen would be done in birch, a pale yet warm wood, with a matching work top. Of course, Tony had then pointed out that his fridge was as outdated as his present Formica, and had sent images of new models that would fit in the available space.

Harry couldn't wait to see the finished product. More importantly, he couldn't wait to see Tony.

He still clung to Tony's words, three days after he'd uttered them. His dream guy? Once the initial shock had worn off, what remained was a sense of peace that Harry had never before encountered. This was real. This was Tony declaring—okay, not in the most romantic of terms, but fuck, he *was* declaring it—that Harry was what he looked for in a partner.

I didn't dream it, did I? Because it had to have been real.

The buzz of his phone announcing a text broke through his thoughts. It was from the vet's surgery, asking him to call them. When Harry got through, he learned the kitten was in good health, which left him with a dilemma. He didn't *have* to do anything: the vet had mentioned taking the kitten to the local RSPCA where they'd keep it until a home could be found.

That was one option. The other was for Harry to keep the kitten.

He had to admit, he liked the idea of coming home to a warm little creature who would curl up in his lap. Then he realized that while Tony could never be described as a little creature, Harry quite liked the idea of coming home to him too, and the thought took him by surprise.

And while he thought about it… Harry scrolled down and called Tony.

"You could've just walked down the street, ya know! That way, I would've got to see you too."

"Sorry, but my lunch break's about to finish. You'll have to wait until later."

"Aww."

Harry laughed. "You're pouting, aren't you?"

"You can hear a pout? Wow. You're good. Okay, why are you calling me, if you're gonna see me later? Not that I'm complaining."

"I called the vet's. One healthy kitten."

"Ooh. Now what? You gonna keep it?" When Harry didn't respond instantly, Tony snickered. "You know you want to. That kitty had 'Harry' written all over it." He paused. "You gonna stop by the vet's surgery after work?"

Harry smiled at the suggestion. "You knew I was going to, right?"

Tony laughed. "I'd have bet money on it. Want me to come with ya? That is, if you wanna see me during the week."

"I see you every day, you barmpot."

Tony guffawed. "Barmpot? Where did that come from?"

"It was one of my grandma's favourite insults. She came from up north. And yes, I want you to come with me." Any excuse to see Tony.

"I'll be waiting at the fence then, same time as usual." Harry caught a muffled shout from the background. "Keep yer 'air on, you bugger! I'm on me break!" He sighed. "Looks like the break is over. Gotta go. See you later, all right?"

"Fine. Go do some work, you lazy git."

Tony's snort filled his ears. "Yeah, love you too." Then he disconnected the call.

Harry stared at his phone, trying to make up his mind about that last casual utterance. But was it just a casual, throwaway phrase?

God, he hoped not.

Tony felt a sense of relief when he saw Harry strolling toward him, bag slung over his shoulder. He appeared a whole lot less uptight than the first time Tony had laid eyes on him, and he hoped the change was something he'd brought about. Certainly, there'd been no sign of the quiet, withdrawn guy from the pub quiz in Harry's bed last Sunday. Even the memory of it was enough to send a shiver down his back.

Harry turns out to be a fucking demon between the sheets.

Only there was more to it than just sex. The prospect of meeting Harry after work had added a lightness to Tony's day, filling it with a sense of expectancy. He'd kept an eye on the time all afternoon, and the closer it came to Harry's finishing time, the more excited Tony became. And one look at the smile that lit up Harry's face when he caught sight of Tony was enough to fill him with a profound feeling of contentment.

"Hey." Harry's voice was soft as he stopped in front of Tony and leaned in to kiss him on the cheek.

"Bugger that," Tony said with a cackle. He cupped Harry's cheek and kissed him on the lips, not bothering to keep it chaste. When they parted, Harry's eyes were bright. Tony sighed contentedly. "I've been waiting all afternoon for that, and I don't fucking care if some old lady mouths off at us for being a pair of fucking perverts."

"Don't mince your words, Tony. Say what you mean." The skin around Harry's eyes crinkled as he grinned.

"An' you need to smile more often. Sexy fucker when you smile." He let go of Harry's cheek and reached for his bag which sat by the fence. "Ready?"

Harry nodded. "I called the surgery and told them to expect us. They close at six-thirty on Wednesdays, so we'd better get a move on." They walked along the street toward the spot where Tony had left his truck.

"Oh. I know what I meant to tell you. A mate of mine called me last night. A week on Saturday, he's having a party. Just a load of friends, a barbecue, a shitload of alcohol. I thought you might wanna come with me." He tried not to watch Harry's expression, anxious not to put pressure on him.

"A party?" The wary note in Harry's voice was unmistakable.

Tony took Harry's hand in his. "A party. Music, booze, cremated burgers and sausages, soggy onions, burnt buns…" He snickered. "The bread variety. It's not that kind of a party." Inside he was already sending out a stream of silent messages. *Go on, Harry, say yes. It'll be fun. Come on, babe…*

After a moment's pause, he got his reply. "Okay."

Tony wanted to yell with triumph, but he managed to temper his jubilation. "Great. We can talk about timing next week. And it'll be casual, a jeans and T-shirts kind of do." He pulled out his keys and unlocked the truck. "Now, is there somewhere we need to go first?"

"Such as?"

"Pets Corner, off Purley Way. I figured you might need some supplies for the new addition to the family. You know, pet carrier, food and water bowls, litter box, kitty bed, brush, not to mention some toys…"

Harry gave a knowing nod. "And now it makes sense. You like cats, don't you? Is that why you're so keen for me to take her home?"

"Cats are good for you. They relieve stress and lower your blood pressure."

"Yeah, and leave little presents all over the house."

Tony could tell by Harry's tone that he wasn't serious. "Well, if we're going, we'd better go now. They close in half an hour."

Harry gaped at him. "And we couldn't have had this conversation in the truck? Get a bloody move on!" He yanked open the passenger door and got in.

Tony laughed and climbed into the truck.

"Look at it this way. By the time I get you to the vet's, you'll need the kitten to calm you down."

He was still smiling to himself as they pulled away from the curb. Tony really liked the direction this relationship was taking.

The receptionist handed Harry the itemised bill. "She's had her shots, and she's also been microchipped as you requested. You'll also have six months' supply of drops to keep her free from fleas and ticks. Kittens as young as eight weeks can be spayed, and the vet thinks she's older than that. You can make an appointment to bring her in for the procedure, but we'd recommend not letting her outdoors until then." She smiled. "We had a lady who came in last week to have her cat done. It turned out to be a dual procedure. Apparently, a neighbourhood cat had got there first."

Tony laughed. "Got any randy tom cats in your street, Harry? If you're not careful, you'll end up with a house full of kittens."

"Not bloody likely," Harry muttered under his breath as he folded the bill and pocketed it. "Do they make kitty chastity belts?"

The receptionist snorted. "Yes. They're called A Locked Door."

At that point, the door to the left opened, and the vet came through, carrying a small bundle of black fur. "Here you go. She's all ready."

"Have you decided on a name for her yet?" the receptionist asked.

Harry nodded. "Star." It was the first thing that had come to him when he saw the little star-like patch of white on her chest. He picked up the pet carrier and opened the gate. "Time to go to your new home, kitty." The vet carefully eased the kitten into the carrier, and Harry fastened the gate. As soon as he put the catch into place, the kitten hooked her claws through the metallic mesh and let out a wail. It was such a plaintive sound it hurt Harry to hear it.

"Let's get her home." Tony took the bag of supplies from the receptionist, who gave him a warm smile when he put his hand to Harry's back.

"I think she's lucky to have two new dads who'll care for her."

It came as something of a shock to Harry to realize he didn't want to be a one-parent family.

As soon as they got through the front door, Tony reached for the box that contained the new litter tray. "Where do you want me to set this up? In the kitchen?"

Harry smirked. "Has she just told you she needs to go? Wow. You learned to speak Cat on the way home? I'm impressed."

"Jerk. This is the first thing you do when you bring a kitten home. You put it on the litter tray so she gets used to where it's located." His eyes sparkled. "Unless you *want* little presents all around the house, in your slippers…." He cocked his head to one side. "Are you a slippers kinda guy, Harry?"

"Have you *seen* any slippers? And go put the

tray down. I don't want to keep her in here any longer than I have to." He'd held onto the carrier while Tony brought in all the pets supplies. Star would want for nothing. She already had enough toys to fill a box, but that was down to Tony. He'd bought several balls in different colours and textures, a laser pointer, and three furry little mice that would probably end up as scraps of fabric, seeing as they were filled with catnip.

Star was going to be one spoiled kitty.

He listened to Tony bustling about in the kitchen. It was on the tip of his tongue to invite him to stay for dinner, except Harry didn't intend on eating anything. If he was going to a party with Tony, he wanted to look his best, and maybe just over a week of eating very little would be enough for him to shed a few pounds. Going with Tony to a bear bar was one thing—a barbecue with Tony's friends was another matter.

Harry wasn't born yesterday. He'd heard enough remarks and caught enough glances to realize people judged him by his appearance. He didn't want to walk into a party and be on the receiving end of a lot of unwanted attention. That would only reflect badly on Tony, and that was the last thing Harry wanted.

Fortunately, fate was on his side.

"Hey, I'd love to stick around for a while, but Mum's making dinner tonight for Tanya and Rocco, and I'm expected." Tony glanced at his phone. "In about ten minutes, so I'd better shift my arse into gear."

Harry widened his eyes. "That sounds like an improvement." He put down the carrier, amid more protests from Star.

"Yeah. She's just working out that Rocco is good for Tanya, so she's had to revise her opinion of Italians." He snickered. "About bloody time." Tony's face straightened. "So, much as I would love to stay here and watch Star wrap you round her little paw, I gotta go. But I'll be here bright and early on Saturday, ready to rip the guts out of your kitchen." He walked over to Harry and kissed him slowly on the mouth. "Just you make sure you have plenty of tea and biscuits to keep me going." Tony leaned in and brushed his lips over Harry's ear. "And don't forget the other essentials. We wouldn't want to run out of them, would we?" He kissed Harry's neck just below his ear, making him shiver.

"You obviously didn't see my shopping list stuck to the fridge door." Condoms was written at the bottom in capital letters.

Tony laughed. "Nice one. And here's a head's up. I'll be wearing as little as possible, because according to the forecast, Saturday's gonna be a scorcher." He waggled his eyebrows. "And that is *not* an invitation to grope me. Too many distractions, and I'll never get it all done in one weekend."

"I'll be on my best behaviour," Harry promised.

Tony stuck out his bottom lip. "You don't have to go *that* far. Just save the manhandling until after I'm done for the day."

In Harry's mind arose an image of Tony in a pair of skimpy shorts, a low-slung tool belt, his bare chest glistening with sweat, his biceps bulging as he hoisted a wall cabinet into position....

Harry was already hot, and it had nothing to do with the climate.

Harry rubbed his eyes and stared blearily at the clock. It was two in the morning, and he was vaguely aware that something had awoken him.

Then he heard it, a mournful sound from downstairs.

Someone was miserable.

Sighing, he climbed out of bed and trudged down the stairs to the kitchen. He pushed open the door and peered into the gloom. A pitiful mewling reached his ears.

Harry assessed his chances of getting a good night's sleep if he left Star where she was, and quickly concluded they were nil. He padded over to the cat basket, feeling for the kitten. "Come 'ere, you." He scooped her up and carried her up to his room. As soon as he set her down on the bed, she padded all over it, examining every inch of the sheet. Harry got back under the covers, and lay on his side, watching her, his eyes heavy with sleep.

Star walked up to him, turned around in a circle, and settled down to sleep, her tail curled around her, paws tucked under her chest.

It wasn't long before Harry joined her.

Chapter Twenty

Harry had to admit, Star was extremely cute. Of course, being woken up by a tiny paw batting your nose was a new experience, and he was thankful her claws were retracted. He'd been in the bathroom when he caught the series of soft *whumps*, and had peered around the door to find Star negotiating the stairs, slowly but with obvious increasing confidence.

She's a fearless little thing.

Once the coffee was brewing, Harry emptied a small can of kitten food into her bowl and set it down next to her water bowl on the new square mat he'd bought for the purpose. About ten minutes later, the sight of her squatting on the kitchen carpet fired an alarm in Harry's head, and he quickly lifted Star onto the litter box. Then he exited the kitchen, reasoning that even kitties needed privacy.

This was all new territory. His parents hadn't had pets when he was growing up, mainly because his mum had been allergic to dog and cat hair. It was slowly dawning on Harry that his new housemate was about to change his life.

Well, it needed changing, right?

By the time he was ready to leave for work, Star was already winding herself in and out of his ankles. Harry reached down to scooch her head. "You have to stay here, kitty. Now, bite the burglars, and don't pee all over the place."

Her yawn might have been a comment.

As Harry closed the front door behind him, he caught movement out of the corner of his eye. Star had climbed over the couch and was sitting in the window, lace curtain covering all of her but her head. Her mouth opened and shut soundlessly, for which Harry was grateful. He wasn't immune to her mournful little mewling.

He walked along the street toward the bus stop, smiling to himself. Knowing she'd spent the day alone meant one thing—he wouldn't hang about when it came time to close the office.

Someone would be waiting for him.

"Hey, not much longer and we'll be outta here," Ben commented as he packed away his tools into his capacious box. "Maybe one more week."

"Yeah." The same thought had been on Tony's mind for the last couple of days.

Ben straightened. "Well, don't sound so happy about it. We'll be working on that new development in Epsom. Plenty to be done there." He closed the tool box and wandered over to where Tony stood by the door that opened out onto a small balcony. "Fuck, mate, who pissed on *your* cornflakes this morning? You've been in a right mood all day."

Tony didn't want to talk about it. "I'm fine," he said shortly. "Let's clear up and get out, yeah? Friday night, and there are beers to be drunk." Not that he felt like drinking. He had a more intimate

activity in mind: a takeaway, a couch, and Harry.
The thought of cuddling up on the couch in front of
the TV would have sounded boring at one point, but
now?

He couldn't think of a better way to spend a
Friday night.

*Guess Harry's not the only one who's
changed.*

Then he reconsidered. As tempting as the
idea was of spending an evening with Harry, he
knew he'd be better off having an early night, to be
ready for the weekend. *There'll be other Friday
nights.* That wasn't a vague hope anymore: Tony felt
it all the way to his bones that he and Harry would
be together for a long while to come.

Now all I have to do is make it a reality.

"Oh, *I* get it now." Ben's amused tone broke
through Tony's internal ramblings.

"Get what?" Tony grabbed his bag. "Are we
goin' or what?" He wouldn't be going home
anyway—he'd sit in his truck until it was time for
Harry to finish work.

"This is all about your fella, ain't it?" Ben's
eyes gleamed. "If you're in Epsom, that means no
more meet-ups after work. No more waitin' by the
fence for 'im to walk past every mornin'." He
pushed out his lower lip. "Aw. Will Tony miss his
big bear?"

"Yes, he fuckin' will," Tony gritted out.
"Happy now?"

Ben stilled. "Mate, Epsom isn't exactly the
ends of the earth, y'know. Half an hour away, a bit
more?" His voice softened. "Boy. You got it bad,
don'tcha?"

Tony knew he was being illogical, but he'd

grown accustomed to seeing Harry every day, even if it was only for a quick morning kiss, or waiting with him at his bus stop. He loved that daily contact, and the idea that he was about to lose it filled him with sorrow.

"Sorry for taking my mood out on you," he said quietly.

"Hey, that's okay. I'm lookin' forward to meeting him next week. You *are* bringin' him to Dezza's party, aren't ya?" Ben wagged his eyebrows. "Gotta show off the new boyfriend, right?"

Tony narrowed his gaze. "I did *not* invite Harry just to have a bloke on my arm, all right? I thought he'd enjoy it. I don't think he goes to many parties." That had to be the understatement of the year. Tony doubted Harry had been to a party this side of his mum dying, and maybe not since he'd moved back home. Maybe that was why Tony was determined to make sure Harry had a good time.

Of course, there *was* the teensiest bit of pride at the thought of Harry being at his side.

"You know what you need to do, don'tcha?" Ben smiled smugly. "Shack up together. It's the obvious solution."

Tony snorted. "Yeah, right. I mean, I've seen *you* move in with a bird when you've known her for all of a month, yeah?" Not that he hadn't had the same thought.

"Yeah, but we're not talkin' about me," Ben remonstrated. "Don't gay guys do shit like that? Act on impulse?"

Tony folded his arms. "I see. You've been making a study of gay men, have ya? Quite the expert. Well, I'm sorry to burst your bubble, but we don't all pop out of the same mould." If he didn't know Ben so well, he'd have been offended by the trite analysis. Actually, it tickled him that Ben had been thinking about Tony's situation.

"Get you. But that doesn't change my opinion. You don't wanna stay at your mum's anyway, do ya? So you and this 'Arry, go find a place of your own." He waggled his eyebrows. "Get all domesticated. Doing the weekly shop together. Feet up in front of the TV, mugs of cocoa…"

Tony guffawed. "Yeah, keep doin' the research, mate. You've still got a lot to learn."

Except there was a part of him that *really* liked those suggestions, not that he would ever tell Ben that.

Tony raised his eyebrows as Harry approached. "What did you do, shove everyone out the door on the dot of five o'clock?"

Harry snickered. "Nothing wrong with good timekeeping. Besides, Star's been on her own all day. I need to get home and find out how much of my house is still in one piece."

Tony snorted. "She's a little kitten. How much damage can she do?"

Harry regarded him steadily. "Claws. Furniture. Carpets." Harry presented his forearm, his sleeve rolled up. Star had caught him there that morning. "Need I say more? And that's without mentioning cat piss and cat poop turning up in various places."

"Good point." Tony twirled his keys on his finger. "Then let me take you home. You'll get there a lot faster." He batted his lashes in an obvious attempt to make Harry laugh.

It worked. "Idiot. Come on then." Harry was in a good mood. The weekend had finally arrived, and he had two days of Tony to look forward to. Another evening with him would just be a bonus.

Just then his stomach growled, and he knew Tony wouldn't let him get away with not eating. Sure enough, Tony peered at him in amusement. "Someone needs their dinner."

"Apparently so." He hastily changed the subject. "So last night was a first." They walked side by side toward Tony's truck.

"Why? What happened?"

Harry grinned. "I shared my bed with a female."

Tony stared at him for a second, then his face creased up with laughter. "Ooh, getting into bad habits already. You're supposed to be the big, strong dad and make her sleep in her basket."

Harry snickered. "Fine. We'll wait until you sleep over this weekend, and see if *you* can put up with her wailing because she doesn't want to be alone downstairs. You'll last five minutes before you cave." He had Tony's number. On the outside he was this rough-and-ready builder, but inside? He was a big softie.

It seems a guy who's soft on the inside is what does it for me.

Tony paused at the truck. "Listen, I'd like to stay tonight—that's assuming I get an invitation…" He sighed. "But I'd better not. I need to be at the building suppliers first thing tomorrow to pick up the stuff, and if I stay with you, I'll just—"

"Get distracted," Harry concluded. He'd had the same thought. "Yeah, that makes sense."

"But that doesn't mean I couldn't stay for a little bit," Tony added, his eyes shining.

"Do I need to ask, a little bit of what?"

Tony laughed out loud. "Anyone ever tell you, you've got a one-track mind?"

"You should know," Harry retorted. "It's a perfect match for yours." For that matter, so was the rest of Tony. "Okay, stay long enough to have a cup of coffee, or dinner, and a cuddle with Star. Because you *know* that's why you're really coming home with me, right?"

Tony's sheepish grin was answer enough.

"Harry?" Tony murmured against his lips.

"Hm?" Harry was busy reacquainting himself with Tony's mouth, because *fuck*, there was nothing like his kisses.

"Your cat is staring at us."

Harry broke off, blinking. "Excuse me?" He sat back and glanced around them. Star was perched on the arm of the couch, tail curled over her front paws, her eyes focused on them. "So she's staring. So what?"

Tony coughed. "Feels weird."

Harry stared at him. "A little kitty watching you with your tongue down my throat is putting you off your stride? Wow." Just then Star yawned and lifted her back leg so she could lick herself. "There.

She's just given us her verdict. We rate less interesting than her little furry bits."

Tony sat up. "I need to go anyway, if I'm gonna be bright-eyed and bushy-tailed tomorrow morning." He cocked his head to one side. "Got the biscuits in?"

Harry laughed. "Yes, greedy guts. You'll be well supplied."

Tony's eyes widened. "What else are you gonna supply with me?" His lips twitched.

"Well, if you don't get your arse out of here sharpish, you won't find out." Harry got to his feet and extended a hand to Tony to pull him up. "Anything I can do to make things a bit easier for you tomorrow?" He'd already emptied the cupboards, placing all their contents in boxes that he'd stored in the rear bedroom, out of the way.

"Have you got a dust sheet?"

Harry frowned. "Possibly. It might be in the garage or the attic." He'd never seen one, however.

"Well, I've got a couple. I'll bring them along. We wanna cover up as much as possible. Take out the kitchen table so I've got space to set up my workbench. But I'm warning ya, dust *will* get everywhere." He smiled. "You'll be blond by the time tomorrow night comes."

Harry smirked. "I've always wondered what I'd look like as a blond." He picked up Tony's bag and handed it to him. "And I'm guessing Star will need to be in her carrier."

Tony nodded. "Can't have her running around the place." He put his arm around Harry's waist and moved closer. "G'night, gorgeous. I'll see you in the morning."

Harry closed his eyes and focused on the kiss

he knew was coming. Tony's lips lingered on his, and Harry put his arms around him, holding him close.

Star's meow had both of them parting, laughing.

"Y'know, for a little thing, she makes a lotta noise," Tony commented, reaching down to stroke Star's head. He bent over until his head was level with hers. "And there's no use being jealous, kitty. You're gonna have to get used to sharing your daddy."

Star yawned, obviously unimpressed.

Tony straightened, and gave Harry a final peck on the lips. "Ain't that right?"

Such possessive language a couple of weeks ago had put Harry's back up. Now?

It warmed him through and through.

"Thanks for staying a while." The idea of dinner had taken a back seat once they'd started making out on the couch. Harry loved that Tony appeared perfectly content to just kiss, and although hands had strayed to crotches now and again, their encounter on the sofa was all the hotter for keeping their clothes on.

That made Harry smile. As a younger man, getting naked had been the be-all, end-all, but there was something definitely sensual about running your hands over fabric, feeling the muscles beneath. It heightened the senses, bringing a heady thrill of anticipation to the proceedings.

Plenty of time for getting naked this weekend. Of that, Harry had no doubt.

"My pleasure," Tony murmured. "And now I really need to go before I change my mind and decide we need to be in your bed right now."

Harry chuckled. "I take it Star stays on the other side of the bedroom door?"

Tony shuddered. "Too right."

"I thought you didn't mind an audience."

He widened his eyes. "I know, right? It doesn't make sense to me either. But having her there…"

Harry thought it endearing. "Okay, no furry spectators. I promise."

Tony kissed him on the tip of his nose. "Yeah, I know, I'm weird. Love me, love my weirdness."

That was the moment it first occurred to Harry that while Tony might have his idiosyncrasies, Harry did in fact love him.

In one month, Tony had waltzed his way into Harry's life, and ultimately found his way to Harry's heart. An event that registered in Harry's mind as a fucking miracle.

Chapter Twenty-One

Tony had been right about one thing—there was dust *everywhere*, mostly from his saw as he trimmed the wall cabinets to get them to fit perfectly. Harry was amazed by how much storage space he'd gained. He particularly liked the cupboard with the glass door: his wine glasses would look great behind that. Some of his glassware had belonged to his grandma, and his mum had instilled in Harry at an early age that he was to be careful around the delicate champagne glasses with their gold rims.

He stood in the doorway, watching Tony, transfixed.

Tony turned his head and gave a loud cough. "I'd hate to cross a desert with you."

Harry knew what that meant. He picked up the kettle and took it over to the sink, skirting around the piles of cabinet doors. They'd be the last thing to go on, Tony had explained. "Tea or coffee?"

"Ooh, tea, please. Nice an' strong."

Harry switched the kettle on and stood next to the sink, admiring the view. Tony had his back to him, and the sight was glorious. He wore heavy boots, and the tightest pair of denim shorts Harry had ever seen. He could see the curve of Tony's arse, and resisted the urge to reach under the frayed hems to stroke him there.

Tony had been right about something else,

too. The day was blisteringly hot, and he had all the windows open to let in the slightest breeze. August was going out with a bang.

The thought made him smile. *Bang*. Tony's dirty mind was rubbing off on him.

Tony stretched his arms above his head, his muscles rippling across his back and shoulders. "Perfect timing, by the way. I'm just ready for a break."

Harry admired his work ethic. Tony had arrived at nine o'clock, and after sharing one good morning kiss, he'd proceeded to unload his truck. He'd only stopped twice in the last six hours, and that had been to grab a sandwich from his cool bag, and to have a cup of coffee at two.

Harry couldn't resist a moment longer. He walked over and trailed his fingers down Tony's back, the surface slick with perspiration. "Have you any idea how sexy you look right now?"

Tony turned around slowly, and Harry wasn't surprised to find his shorts unfastened, revealing dark fuzz. *Fuck*. That did it every time. Harry's cock sat up and took interest.

Tony snickered. "You wanna be careful. This sounds like dialogue from one of those cheesy 70s films. *You* know, Adventures of a window cleaner…" He licked his lips. "Adventures of a builder." He grinned. "Wanna see my plumb bob?"

Harry chuckled. "Is this where I say my husband's going to be away for hours?"

"*Now* you're gettin' it." Tony cupped his crotch, where his dick was already pushing again the zipper. "Wanna see my multi-tool?"

"Oh, is *that* what you're calling it now?" Harry stretched out his hand to one of Tony's power tools that was sitting on the draining board. "What's this?"

"That's my impact driver." Tony waggled his eyebrows. "It's got a nice drill too."

"Do you need drilling?" Harry asked playfully.

Tony stilled, and the hairs on Harry's arms stood on end as if the air had suddenly become electrically charged. "You can drill me anytime." The husky, raw quality to his voice sent a shiver skating down Harry's back. Then he grinned again, his face alight. "And I *am* on a break, right?"

Harry was grinning too. "Now tell me you have condoms in your tool box, and I'll believe you were a Boy Scout."

Tony's eyes sparkled. "As a general rule, no, but just for today, yeah. Lube too."

That was all Harry needed to know.

He slid his hands around Tony's waist, and their mouths collided in a heated kiss, tongues plunging deep. Tony's skin was warm beneath his fingertips.

"Upstairs?" Tony managed to gasp out between kisses.

"Too far. Living room." Thank God for dust sheets. Tony had covered everything in sight.

Tony let out a throaty chuckle. "Who's doin' who?"

Harry paused long enough to grin again. "I'm thinking flip-fuck."

"*Nice.*" Tony's long, drawn-out sound of appreciation did masses for Harry's self-esteem. He grabbed Harry by the hand and started tugging him out of the kitchen, until he halted, let go of Harry, and lunged toward the tool box that stood next to the sink unit. "Wait!" He rummaged around before triumphantly holding up a sachet of lube and a couple of shiny condom packages. "*Now* I'm ready." He gaped at Harry. "You're still dressed?"

"So are you," Harry retorted, but even as he said the words, Tony was shoving his denim shorts down over his muscular thighs, his dick bouncing up. He kicked them off, then raised his eyebrows.

"Well, get a bloody move on. This arse won't fuck itself, y'know."

Harry laughed. "I wouldn't put it past you to have tried, what with the size of your cock." He left the kitchen, Tony right behind him. By the time Tony had pulled the curtains, Harry's T-shirt lay on the floor, and he was already pulling off his jeans.

Tony was chuckling. "Doesn't every gay boy try that at one point?"

Harry decided to keep quiet on that subject. He pointed to the couch. "Face the back." This was going to be hard and fast.

Tony complied, kneeling on the covered seat cushions, his legs spread wide, arse tilted in offering. He glanced over his shoulder as he rested his arms on the back of the couch. "What, no foreplay?" He was still grinning.

Harry picked up the sachet of lube from where Tony had left it on the seat, tore it open, and slicked up a couple of fingers. "Here. I'll give you foreplay." He spread Tony's cheeks with one hand and was about to penetrate that inviting hole when Tony reached back to grip his wrist.

"Where's the cat?"

Harry snorted. "Relax, will you? She's upstairs, in her carrier. And I don't want to think about cats. Not when all I can think about is *this*."

And with that, he slid his fingers into Tony's body.

Tony groaned. "Christ, what thick fingers you have."

Harry leaned over Tony's back and whispered, "All the better to fuck you with." God, sex had *never* been this much fun.

"Then don't hang about," Tony flung back at him. "Hurry up and fuck me with 'em."

Harry had no problem with following instructions. He moved his fingers deeper, until he was in up to the knuckle, and Tony's breathing was loud and harsh. "Like that?"

"God, yes." Tony dug his fingers into the sheet, gripping it tightly. "Thank fuck I brought sheets and not plastic. Nothing worse than fucking on plastic. It sticks to everything—and I mean *everything*." Harry withdrew his fingers, only to plunge them deep into Tony's heat, and Tony threw his head back. "Oh, fuck, yeah."

"I can do this for as long as you want," Harry promised, sliding faster now.

To his surprise, Tony reached back, and grabbed him around the wrist again, pulling him free. "Yeah, but I want some fun too." He got off the couch and pushed Harry onto it on his back. "My turn."

Harry's heart pounded as Tony slicked up his fingers. "Oh, God, yeah." He hooked his arms under his knees and drew them up toward his chest, baring his hole to Tony's view. "Get 'em in there."

"With pleasure." Tony knelt on the couch, copying Harry's action of a moment earlier. He spread Harry's arse, smiling. "Fucking love this hole." And before Harry could growl at him to *fucking get a move on*, Tony's fingers filled him to the hilt.

Christ, the burn was delicious.

Harry's skin tingled and despite the heat, icy shivers crawled through him. He drew his knees up higher, rolling his arse up off the couch, and Tony responded by not wasting any time. He crooked his finger, and Harry felt the connection instantly.

"Yeah, there it is," Tony said almost gleefully. "Fancy a little internal massage?"

"Only if it's your dick doing the massaging," Harry fired back, his need increasing with every stroke of Tony's fingers inside him.

Tony's wide grin was enough to inform Harry he was about to get what he asked for.

"Think I can manage that." Tony picked up both condoms and dropped one on Harry's belly. "And yeah, that's a hint."

Harry lost no time in sheathing his cock. The way the afternoon was shaping up, it was anyone's guess which of them got to bury their dick first in a tight hole.

Which was fucking perfect, as far as Harry was concerned.

Tony loved it when sex was less by rote, and more energetic and organic. And this was shaping up to be a rough-and-ready, go-with-the-flow quickie. It was a side to Harry he hadn't seen before, and it went a long way to cementing what Tony already knew.

Harry was perfect for him.

Musing while putting on a Johnny meant distraction, however, and it amused him that Harry chose that moment to take the lead, scrambling up off the couch and shoving Tony until he was bent over the sheeted coffee table. Not that Tony was resisting, exactly.

Tony was having a ball.

"Spread for me." The gruff note in Harry's voice sent a shudder through him, and Tony widened his legs, his hands propping him up. He quickly realized that first slow press of Harry's cock inside him was all the finesse he was going to get, because once Harry buried his dick to the hilt, he grabbed hold of Tony's hips and got down to fucking him in earnest. Tony dropped his head and stared at the view beneath: his own cock, rigid, pointing along his body like an arrow; and Harry's thick thighs moving as he slammed into Tony, his balls hanging low. Added to that were the grunts and other sexy as fuck noises that poured out of Harry as he truly let himself go.

"Love… the way…. you fuck me," Tony gasped out. He lifted his head, closed his eyes, and pushed back onto Harry's dick that was spearing into him. "C'mon, Harry, fuck me like you mean it. Show me what you're made of."

"You mean… like this?" Harry drove his cock deep, punching the air from Tony's lungs.

"Holy fuck, yeah. Again." Tony couldn't keep still, impaling himself again and again, loving the slide of hot flesh into him. When Harry pulled out, he wanted to howl—until he straightened and saw him bent over the arm of the couch, his gaze focused on Tony, his eyes dark.

Oh yeah.

Tony squeezed out what was left of the lube, aimed his cock at Harry's glistening pink hole, and thrust into him, hands free.

"Oh, that's it." Harry's head hit the seat cushions, while he reached back to spread his arse. "Yeah, like that. Balls deep."

Tony eased out of him and nearly came at the sight of that dark, stretched hole, just waiting for more. "Fucking hungry arse." He plunged deep, filling Harry in one hot thrust, then proceeded to do it again, and again, until Harry was reduced to one or two words interspersed with gasps and moans. "Yeah, you like a rough fuck, don'tcha? Love feeling that fat dick inside you, stretching you wide?"

"Fuck, yeah. And if you keep hitting that spot, I'm gonna come in less than a minute," Harry groaned.

"That's fine." Tony fucked him with short, quick thrusts, knowing from the way Harry's shivers intensified that he was hitting it all right. "I've got a kitchen to finish, remember? Besides, there's always tonight, right?" He set up another punishing rhythm, flesh slapping loudly against flesh.

"How… can you… think about kitchens…when you're… fucking?" Harry arched his back, tilting his arse even higher.

"Why do you think I haven't come yet? I'm visualizing sawing… cutting… anything but screwing."

"How about riding?" Harry twisted to look at him. "How does that sound?"

Tony was out of him in a second. "Give me a cock to sit on an' I'll show ya."

Harry was off the arm and onto the seat

cushions in a heartbeat.

"Fuck, you can move fast."

Harry held his shaft steady and grinned. "For a bear, you mean? Now park your arse on this."

Tony straddled him, squatting into a sitting position above Harry's dick.

"That's it. Hold onto the couch and let me do the driving."

Tony snickered. "Didn't know you drive." He let out a sigh of pleasure as the head of Harry's cock kissed his hole. "Yeah, in me."

"Oh, I know what goes where." Harry's gaze locked onto his as he leisurely thrust up. He cradled Tony's arse in both hands. "Start slowly, just moving up and down on my dick. Want to kiss you before we build up for the finale."

Tony had no problems with kissing.

Harry tilted his head back and their mouths met, tongues instantly in play, while Harry alternately squeezed and stroked Tony's arse cheeks as Tony filled himself again and again.

"On your knees," Harry whispered. Tony changed position, kneeling over him, still holding onto the couch. He rocked back and forth on Harry's cock, Harry helping him, his hands still on Tony's cheeks. Then both of them were moving in harmony, Harry pushing up into him while Tony pushed back to meet his thrusts. No words, just the sound of their mingled breathing, growing more rapid with each exquisite glide of Harry's cock inside him.

It was too good to last.

Tony fumbled with the latex, trying to free his dick, and at last he was tugging on his bare shaft, his orgasm locked in place, assured, nothing to stop it as he shot his load over Harry's chest, still moving. He let out a soft cry, the pleasure spilling out of him, loving the feel of Harry's hands on his waist and back, arse and thighs, a constant reminder of his presence.

Harry focused on Tony's face. "My turn," he said softly, before moving again inside him, only gently now, as if trying to hold on to the bliss he was so obviously feeling for just that bit longer.

Tony brought their mouths together once more, his body still shivering from the waves of physical satisfaction that continued to crash into him at intervals. "Wanna feel you come inside me," he murmured against Harry's lips.

Harry locked his mouth on Tony's, and a shudder ran the length of his body.

"Yeah, that's it," Tony encouraged him. Harry trembled beneath him, and Tony closed his eyes, waiting for that tell-tale throb inside him. When it came, he buried his face in Harry's beard, loving the soft rasp against his cheek.

They sat there for a moment, Tony's arms around Harry's neck, Harry's arms around Tony's waist, their lips fused in kiss after gentle kiss. A pitiful meow came from above their heads, and Tony inclined his face toward the ceiling.

"And you can shut up an' all."

Harry opened his eyes wide. "Aw. She's been up there all day on her own. Be nice."

Tony snickered. "I *was* nice. And relax, I love the little furball." He winked. "Just not when we're fucking, all right?" He stroked Harry's beard. "She can still sleep on the bed. I'm not *that* intimidated by her."

"Of course not." Harry smirked. "You just don't like the idea of her holding up a score card and rating you on your performance."

"And how much would I have got for just now?"

Harry kissed him, a lingering, sensual kiss that made Tony's toes curl. "Twelve out of ten?"

"Ooh, if that's the case, I'll have to come here more often."

Harry's eyes had those flecks of emerald again. "Come as often as you like."

Tony's half-hard dick gave a twitch. "Now that's an invitation I'll definitely be taking you up on."

Except it wasn't the invitation he wanted, and he knew it.

He lifted himself gingerly off Harry's now limp cock, and stood beside him, hand outstretched. "Come on. We'll have a quick shower before I finish off for the day. Then we can sit on the couch all night and cuddle." He peered at it. "Once I've removed the sheets." He hoisted Harry to his feet, and was disturbed when Harry lost his balance for a moment. "Hey. You all right?"

Harry blinked a couple of times, then nodded. "I got up too quickly. All the blood must have rushed to my head."

"Yeah, well, it had a way to travel. Most of it was in your dick." He peered closely at Harry. "Are you sure you're okay? You're a little pale. And usually, afterwards, you're... well... flushed."

Harry snickered. "Thanks, *Dr*. Valverde. I'm fine. Sticky, but fine. And seeing as that is entirely down to you, I think you should be the one to clean me off."

Tony's eyes lit up. "Wash cloth—or tongue?"

Harry rolled his eyes. "Bathroom. Because I'm sure I've got sawdust sticking to me, and if that gets anywhere painful, you've had it." He swatted Tony's arse. "Upstairs."

Tony laughed and walked out of the room, heading for the stairs, Harry behind him. As he climbed them, he reasoned that if it was more than momentary dizziness, Harry would tell him.

At least, Tony hoped he would.

Chapter Twenty-Two

Tony smacked his lips. "You can't beat fish and chips eaten right out of the paper. And I love Castella's cod."

Harry had to admit, the food was delicious. It had been Tony's idea, once he'd wrapped up for the day, and Harry got the impression he wasn't going to take no for an answer. Besides, how could he resist the lure of fish and chips?

Star had been pretty interested too. Her little nose had twitched the minute Tony entered the house, and Harry had laughed to see her following him to the kitchen. When they sat down on the couch to eat, their opened packages spread out on trays, two little paws appeared on the edge of the seat cushion, followed by the rest of Star a split second later. After receiving small bits of flaked cod, first from Harry, then from Tony, she was returned to her basket.

Tony scrunched up the wad of white paper that had contained his dinner, now transparent in places where the oil had soaked through. He held out his hand for Harry's, then took both lots through into the kitchen. A takeaway had been the obvious alternative: Harry's kitchen wasn't ready to deal with food preparation. Another day, Tony assured him, and he wouldn't recognize it.

Of course, he *might* have achieved a little more if they hadn't stopped to fuck each other's brains out, but where was the fun in that?

Tony leaned against the door jamb. "So… we goin' out or stayin' in?"

Harry knew exactly what he wanted to do, but as to whether Tony would be receptive, he had no clue. *Maybe it's about time I found out.*

He cleared his throat. "Actually? I'd prefer to stay in. I was going to watch an episode of… Strictly." He waited. Millions of viewers might tune in avidly for every series of Strictly Come Dancing, but that didn't mean Tony was one of them.

Tony frowned. "But… it's not on now."

Harry coughed. "I know. I've got them recorded on my hard drive."

"Really? How many episodes?"

Another cough. "Four series." He paused. "I mean, it's not like I have them *all*, right? Because that would be fifteen series, and that's just… nuts. But yeah, I've recorded a few."

Tony's eyes gleamed. "Which series was Ben Cohen in?"

Harry gave a knowing smile. "Eleven. And I've got it."

"You got any beer in the house?"

Harry shook his head. "But there's a bottle of red wine in the cupboard under the stairs." It had been sitting there for at least a month.

"Perfect. That'll do. I'll crack it open, you find us some glasses, and then we can settle down for a night of ogling Ben Cohen's moves."

Harry went over to the cabinet to fetch the glasses. "Do you think he's good looking?" He knew it was stupid to be anxious—especially after what they'd been doing that afternoon—but he couldn't help his reaction.

Tony yelled from the kitchen, "Where's the corkscrew? Sod it. Never mind, I'll improvise." A couple of minutes later, he returned with an open bottle of wine, still smiling. "I'd be lost without my tool box. Did you say something? I missed it, 'cause I was hunting for a bloody corkscrew."

"I asked if you thought Ben Cohen was good looking."

Tony snorted. "He's not a gay pinup for nothing." He put the bottle down on the coffee table, then straightened. "Yeah, he's a looker, but why settle for *lomo de cerdo* when you can have *filete de vaca*?"

Harry gazed at him inquiringly. "Do I get a translation?"

Tony walked around the table and stopped in front of Harry. "Why settle for pork steak when you can beef fillet?" He leaned in and kissed Harry on the mouth, a slow, chaste kiss that sent warmth spreading through him.

When they parted, Harry gave him an inquiring glance. "So... I'm steak?"

Tony waggled his eyebrows. "Prime beef, babe, all the way through." He sat down on the couch and stretched out his long, bare legs. The plain black shorts were all he wore, which was understandable, given the evening temperature. Harry liked that Tony wasn't *all* muscles: there was the hint of a tummy above the waistband.

"Harry? Wanna find the recording?" Tony's amused voice broke through, and he gave himself a mental shake.

"Sorry. Zoned off for a second there."

Tony snickered. "Probably thinking about Ben Cohen."

Suddenly it was important to set the record straight. "You. I was thinking about you."

Silence, and then Tony smiled, the skin around his eyes crinkling. "We're even then. I'm always thinking about you." Their gazes met, and Harry lost himself in a pair of deep brown eyes. "Now, while you find the right spot on the hard drive, I'll fetch the kitty from the hallway." Another smile. "Can't have her stuck out there all night while we're in here, right? She'll miss out on all the cuddles." He left the room.

Harry had to smile. He loved this side of Tony. About as much as he loved the rest of him.

Harry checked the front door was locked and everything switched off before climbing the stairs. When he reached the bedroom door, he paused, listening.

"Yeah, you're a cute little thing, aren't ya? And yeah, you can stay here, but here's the rule. If your daddy and me wanna play, off the bed you go."

Harry laughed and peered around the door. Tony glanced up from the bed where he lay beneath a single sheet. Star was on her back on the bed beside him, both front paws grabbing onto his arm, her back feet pushing at him. Harry watched in frank amusement. "And you say she has *me* wrapped around her little paw?" He chuckled. "You all done with the bathroom?"

"Yup." Tony returned his attention to Star, who was butting his hand with her head. "Aw, I'm sorry. Did I stop paying attention to you, little girl?"

Harry left them and went to clean his teeth. As he studied his reflection in the mirror, it occurred to him that having Tony there felt totally normal, as though he belonged. Okay, so he'd lived alone since his mum had died, and yes, there were times when he realized he was lonely, but this wasn't simply a case of Tony conveniently filling a void.

Tony was a good fit in his life. Tony *belonged* there. And the worse thing he could think of right then was losing him.

I don't want this to end.

His ablutions finished, he clicked off the light and returned to the bedroom. Tony gave him an appreciative stare. "You're lookin' good, do you know that? I mean, you've *always* looked good to me, but yeah, maybe you're looking better." He gave him a knowing smile. "What's your secret?"

The first thing to flit through Harry's mind was that the 'fasting' was finally paying off, not that he was about to share *that*. Then another thought snuck its way in there, and he had to bite back the words to keep them from spilling out.

Love. That's my secret. Loving you makes me look good.

In the end, he went with humour. "I've got a painting in the attic." Harry climbed into bed, and Tony covered him with the sheet. Harry switched off the bedside lamp, and semi-darkness enveloped them.

Tony snorted. "Yeah, well, get that gorgeous arse over here, Dorian Gray. I wanna fall asleep with you in my arms tonight."

Harry had absolutely no problem with that.

He lay on his side, Tony curled around his

back, his arm over Harry's waist, his hand resting over Harry's heart. The soft *whump* that greeted his ears had to be Star jumping off the bed. *Maybe three's a crowd for a kitty.* He didn't think for a minute that she'd stray all that far from the bed.

"Should be nice for the party next weekend," Tony said quietly, before kissing Harry's shoulder. "You're gonna have a great time. Can't wait to introduce you to my friends."

A thought struck him. "And who will you be introducing me as?"

Tony snuggled closer, if that were possible. "Harry, my fella. My boyfriend. Whatever works for ya." He kissed Harry's neck. "'Cause that's what you are, right? My man?"

Harry covered Tony's hand with his and squeezed it gently. "Yeah, your man." He closed his eyes and prayed fervently that he was more than the current man. He wanted to be *the* man.

Tony took a last glance around, nodding in satisfaction. *Perfect.*

"Can I come in now?" The wistful note in Harry's voice made him smile even more. He'd kept Harry out of the kitchen all day, determined to do a final reveal when it was all finished.

Tony laughed and opened the door. "Ta-daaa!"

Harry stepped into the room almost nervously, then came to a halt, his mouth open. "Bloody hell."

And right there, Tony felt wonderful. "You like it, then?" He'd given the task everything he'd got, and he had to admit, it looked fantastic. A kitchen he'd be proud to call his own.

Harry's face glowed. "Like it? It's… amazing. I can't believe it's the same room."

What took Tony by surprise was the sudden hug.

He chuckled. "Yeah, it's safe to say you like it."

Harry released him and walked over to the work surfaces, running his hands carefully over the wood. "This is beautiful. And the birch gives the whole room a gorgeous light." He marvelled at the look of it. "Really, it looks nothing like it did." His eyes sparkled. "Now all I have to do is bring the rest of the house up to this standard. I had no idea it'd be such a… transformation."

Tony knew exactly what he meant. "I was just thinking to myself that I'd love a kitchen like this myself."

"Do you do much cooking at home?"

He sighed. "How much do you *think* I get to do with a mother like mine? I'm lucky if I get to make a piece of toast, which is a pity, because I'd love to do more cooking."

Just then his phone vibrated in his pocket. Tony took it out and groaned when he saw the screen.

"What's the matter?"

"Mum texting me to call her is *never* a good thing." He clicked on her number, his heart sinking. Ten to one, this would mean having to leave Harry's earlier than he'd planned. "Mamá? *Qué pasa?*"

"Did you forget something?" Her voice was

quiet, always a danger signal.

"I don't know—did I?" He had no clue.

"Your Aunt Marisa is coming to stay with us, remember, while the council does repairs on her block of flats?"

Oh shit. "And you asked me to clear out Tanya's old room." Damn it. He'd completely forgotten, what with all the plans to work at Harry's.

"Ah, so you *do* remember. Well, she'll be here in a couple of hours, and I wouldn't ask a *dog* to stay in that room, let alone my sister. I thought you'd done it, but I just went to check, and—"

"Yeah, yeah, I get it." Tony got it, all right. He'd fucked up. "I'll be there as quick as I can, okay?" He didn't wait for her response but disconnected the call.

Harry regarded him with compassion. "Are you in trouble?"

Tony rolled his eyes. "When am I not? It's one thing after another lately. I tell you, I am getting out of there as soon as I can. Never mind waiting until I've got enough for my own place. I'll rent the first flat I can find. Anything, as long as it has a roof and four walls." He gave Harry a peck on the cheek. "Sorry, babe, but I gotta run. Thank God I've already packed the tools away, eh? I'll see you in the morning."

Harry followed him to the front door. "Don't drive like a maniac, okay? Be safe."

That brought him to a standstill. Tony turned around and kissed him, taking his time. "I'll be safe. And thanks for thinking about me." With that, he unlocked the truck, got in, and reversed carefully out of Harry's driveway.

As he headed toward the turning, Tony

gritted his teeth. *I will* not *be living at home when I hit thirty-one, and that's a promise.*

Harry watched until Tony was out of sight, then slowly closed the door.

Not exactly how I wanted the day to end, but hey…

He walked through into the kitchen and marvelled yet again at Tony's workmanship. *He's really good at what he does.* Harry's seventies-style room had been transformed into something that wouldn't look out of place in the pages of an interior design magazine. It was the kind of kitchen made for cooking, not that Harry ever cooked.

Then maybe it's time I started. Not to do so, when given such a space, seemed a crime.

Poor Tony. Harry's heart went out to him. It was obvious he hated living with his mum, and it seemed cruel that only finances kept him there.

Then do something about it.

Harry stared at the kitchen window, unseeing. There *was* a solution—if he was prepared to step out of his comfort zone and into new territory. Only two things gave him pause. One, he had no idea what Tony's reaction would be to what was undoubtedly a huge and possibly hasty proposal. And two?

He was scared to death, because this would change everything.

Maybe some more thinking was required before he took a step off into the deep end.

Chapter Twenty-Three

By Thursday, Harry was beginning to think fasting was not the way to go.

It had been Tony's comment that had given him the idea. If Harry was looking better, then it was likely to be a result of his difference in—or lack of—diet, and that was incentive enough to continue. After all, he had a party to attend.

Sunday night, he'd sat on the couch, reading online articles about keto fasting and how it was the way to go to give your weight loss a boost. It was only then that he realized what he'd been doing so far virtually amounted to fasting. Why not give it a 'boost' by following advice and having three or four days of solid fasting? He'd coped thus far, right?

Except this time, he'd begun to notice a few things that could have been directly linked to the fasting. For one, he felt tired. Not all the time, but more than usual. Then there were the headaches—or was it the same headache that simply kept coming back? And as for any enthusiasm toward his work? His get-up-and-go had got up and gone.

Harry knew he'd been more irritable during the last few days. He'd snapped at Deb unnecessarily, and the hurt look in her eyes had mortified him. A bottle of wine and a bunch of flowers the following day had mollified her, and Harry had spent the rest of the day watching his Ps and Qs.

He'd expected to be ravenous, but what

surprised him were the sugar cravings that had recently developed. Harry had never had much of a sweet tooth, but walking past the local sweet shop had become sheer torture.

Maybe this is not such a good idea. If this was what the fasting was doing to him, was it worth it? By the time he was due to finish work on Thursday, he'd reached a few decisions. No more fasting. More exercise. Sensible eating. Fewer takeaways.

One by one, the staff said goodnight and filed out of the building, until only Harry and Simon remained. In fact, Simon seemed unaware that everyone had gone. Harry picked up his bag and walked slowly over to Simon's desk. Christ, he felt so lethargic. It was as if his limbs were encased in lead. He reached the desk and leaned against it, amused to find Simon so obviously engrossed in his work.

Harry cleared his throat, and Simon almost hit the ceiling.

"For God's sake, don't sneak up on me like that, Harry!" Then he glanced around him. "Where'd everybody go?"

Harry snickered. "Home, Oh Observant One. Which is where you and I will be heading any second now, if I can tear you away from that computer."

Simon grimaced as he saved his work. "I've been revamping this woman's CV. Honestly, some people have no clue how to sell themselves."

Harry gazed at him proudly. Simon had rapidly become one of his best staff. "Well, you can finish it tomorrow. Then have a well-deserved break at the weekend."

"Yeah." Simon got to his feet and slung his bag over his shoulder. "Right now, there's an ice-cold glass of Chardonnay calling my name somewhere, and I'm gonna hunt it down."

"You do that." Harry headed for the door, but came to a halt when a wave of dizziness crashed over him, causing him to stumble, almost falling over his own feet.

"Harry?" Simon was at his side in an instant, his hand on Harry's arm. "Are you all right? You've gone a funny colour. Let me—"

Whatever else Simon said was lost as Harry's legs suddenly became incapable of holding him upright, and he fell toward the floor, the world blackening out before he hit it.

"Harry. *Harry*!"

Simon's voice seemed to be echoing through a veil of fog. Harry blinked a couple of times, and put his hand to his head, which ached like a bastard. Then he realized he was on the floor.

"What the hell?"

Simon was kneeling beside him. "Don't move. Stay where you are." He looked so serious. "Now, have you got any pain in your neck?"

Harry lifted his head off the floor, and the world swam. "Oh God." He lowered it again. "Tell the room to stop moving. And I just feel dizzy. Well, that and a headache, but I've had one of those all day."

"You fainted. And you're gonna stay right there until you're not dizzy anymore, you hear me?"

Simon scraped a hand through his hair. "Fuck, you scared me. There was no way I could've caught you, you dropped so fast. And I can't lift you up, so you need to just lie there until—" He broke off and stared at the door, his eyes wide. "Don't move! I'll be right back." Then he scrambled to his feet, ran to the door, flung it open, and he was gone.

Harry stared after him in disbelief. What the fuck?

Tony glanced at his phone. Harry was a little later than usual, but he didn't mind waiting. The job finished the following day, so he'd take every minute he could get.

He looked up at the sound of someone running toward him. It was the twink who worked with Harry. Tony's gut knotted up. *Harry…*

"You're Harry's bloke, aren't you?" the young man said breathlessly as he reached Tony.

"What's happened?" Tony's heartbeat sped up. "Something wrong with Harry?"

The young man nodded vigorously. "Come with me."

Tony didn't need telling twice.

They ran to the recruitment office, Tony running ahead of the guy. When he pushed open the door and saw Harry lying on the floor, cold flushed through him in an icy rush. He dashed over and knelt beside him. "Harry?"

"I'm okay, so stop panicking before you give yourself a heart attack." Harry took a deep breath. "I just had a dizzy spell, that's all."

"He fainted," the young man blurted out. "I told him to stay put."

Harry glared at him. "And you went to get Tony?"

Simon glared right back. "Well, I said I couldn't lift you, didn't I? But your fella, *he* can."

"Quick thinking," Tony told him. "What's your name again? I mean, we haven't been introduced." He was doing his best to stay calm.

"I'm Simon. Sorry if I scared you, running up to you like that, but you were the only one I could think of." He squatted down next to Harry. "Think you can make it to a chair if we help you?"

Harry narrowed his gaze. "It was just a dizzy spell."

"Yeah, right." Tony returned his narrow gaze. "And you *just* fainted, I suppose." He glanced at Simon. "Drag that chair over here, will ya? I'll lift him up."

"I *am* here, y'know."

Harry's gruff tone went a long way to quelling Tony's panic. He softened his voice. "Yeah. Thank God. Now let me help you, you stubborn sod." Simon moved a chair close to them, and Tony moved into position, hooking his arms under Harry's. "Gently, now. Take your time." Simon held out his hands, Harry took them, and between them they got him seated. Tony peered at his face. Harry was a little pale, but he met Tony's gaze, his eyes focused on Tony's face. That steady observation was what finally let Tony relax.

He's all right. For the moment anyway. Tony still wanted to know what had caused the dizziness. Saturday's brief moment of instability now seemed suspect.

Time enough for questions when I get him home.

"Okay, you're gonna stay here while I go and fetch the truck, right? Simon will stay with you. That okay?" He flicked a glance in Simon's direction, who responded with an emphatic nod. "Then I'm gonna take you home."

"I'm all right, honest. I think you're making a fuss over nothing," Harry protested.

Tony levelled a keen glance at him. "You can think what you want. People don't faint for no reason. And you're gonna let me take care of you. No arguments." He straightened, and reached into his pocket for his keys. "I'll be back in a minute." He caught Simon's gaze. "Could you bring him a glass of water, please? And don't let him move out of that chair until I get back."

Simon smiled. "You got it." He folded his arms across his slim chest. "He's going nowhere."

Satisfied, Tony bent down and gave Harry a peck on the cheek, before heading out the door. Once outside, he walked briskly toward his truck.

Okay, Harry, what the hell is going on?

Chapter Twenty-Four

By the time Tony pulled into Harry's street, Harry was feeling very foolish.

Can't believe I fainted. Grown men didn't faint. Except he knew what might have caused it. And although Tony hadn't said as much, Harry had a sinking feeling he'd want to discuss it.

He had to hand it to Simon. The lad had thought fast. Much as Harry hated the idea of Tony seeing him like that, it had been good to have him there.

"You okay to get into the house, or do you need an arm?"

Harry hadn't even registered that the engine had stopped. Tony was regarding him, a thoughtful look in his eyes.

"I can manage, thanks." Harry climbed out of the truck and walked carefully up to his front door. Tony wasn't far behind him. Once inside, Tony headed for the kitchen.

"I'm putting the kettle on. And *you* are gonna sit on the couch," he called out.

Harry huffed. "Bossy sod, aren't you?"

Tony appeared in the kitchen doorway, his expression serious. "When it comes to taking care of you, too right I'm bossy. And right now it's bleedin' obvious you need taking care of. So, shoes off, sit down, then you an' me are gonna have a little chat."

Shit. Harry considered putting him off, using

his headache as an excuse. Not that he needed one—the dull ache hadn't left him. But he knew Tony. *And admit it, hasn't it felt wrong having to lie about meals and food shopping these last few weeks?* Maybe it was time for truth between them, especially if he wanted this relationship to work.

He dropped his bag onto the floor below the hall mirror, kicked off his shoes and placed them on the rack, then went into the living room. By the time he'd sat down, Tony was there with a steaming mug, which he placed in front of Harry on the coffee table.

"Hot, sweet tea. And no complaints, mister. Just drink it." Tony left the room.

"Your bedside manner needs a bit of work. Just saying," he shouted toward the kitchen. Inwardly he loved the way Tony took charge of the situation. Harry had never needed someone to lean on; it had always been the other way around. He rested his head against the back of the couch and closed his eyes, wondering how he could explain his reasons for his actions.

He is not *going to be happy*. That much was a given.

After a few minutes, Tony came into the room, and Harry opened his eyes. "You going to join me?"

Tony nodded and sat down beside him, a mug of tea in his hand. "So, any theories as to why you came over all dizzy?"

Harry took a deep breath. "Yeah, well, about that…"

"What did you have for breakfast?"

The abrupt question stilled him, and Harry regarded Tony with apprehension. "The usual."

Tony gazed at him speculatively. "And that

would be, what? Toast? Cereal? Stuff like that?"

"Yes. Well, no. I mean—" Harry's pulse quickened.

"Wanna explain to me why your fridge is virtually bare? Apart from a butter dish and your ground coffee, there's nothing in there." Before Harry could respond, he pressed on. "Your cupboards are the same. And I just checked your bin. No evidence that you've eaten anything since Monday. That's when your bins are collected, right? Same as mine? So what the fuck have you been eating, Harry?"

Harry stiffened. "You checked my bins? So you're a detective now? What the bloody hell—"

"No, I'm not a bleedin' detective. *I'm* just someone who's worried to death that you're doing something stupid, and I want to know why!" Tony stared at him with wide eyes.

"It was just a few days' fasting, to help boost my weight loss," Harry said simply. "I've been trying lose weight ever since…." His heart quaked.

"Ever since when?" Tony asked, his voice softer.

Harry bit the bullet. "Since I met you, and we started going out."

Tony blinked. "But… why? You don't need to lose weight. You're fine just as you are."

"Really? Then what was that you said the other night about how I was looking better, and what was my secret?"

Tony became very still. "Wait a minute. You thought by that, I meant you'd lost some weight and you were looking better for it? That's not what I meant at all!" He ran his fingers across his scalp. "Is that why you did the fasting? Because you thought you were obviously on the right track?" Tony wrung his hands. "Has *nothing* I've said this last month gotten through to you? There is *nothing wrong* with the way you look. I fucking *love* the way you look."

"Then what did you mean?" Harry stared at him. "Was it just something to say, to make me feel good?"

"No!" Tony heaved a huge sigh. "All I meant was, you had this… glow about you. Like you were all lit up inside. And I kinda hoped…." Tony bowed his head.

Everything stopped. Harry ceased to hear the clock ticking, the birds chirping, the distant drone of traffic… His focus narrowed onto Tony's face, onto those gorgeous brown eyes. He couldn't speak, for fear his words would jinx whatever was about to come out of Tony's mouth.

What he prayed was about to come out.

Tony raised his head and locked gazes with Harry. "I hoped it was because you were happy being with me. That maybe you were… in love with me."

"You hoped that?" Harry's heartbeat sped up.

Tony smiled. "It only seems fair. Seeing as I'm in love with you." He gazed expectantly at Harry, who had to smile, knowing exactly what he was seeking.

Harry wasn't going to make him wait. "Then isn't it fortuitous that I happen to be in love with you?" He couldn't resist grinning.

Tony rolled his eyes. "Hallebleedinlujah!" He opened his arms wide. "Come 'ere, you beautiful bear."

Harry didn't hesitate. He moved swiftly into

the circle of Tony's strong arms, which enfolded him in a hug. His cheek met Tony's, and he welcomed the rasp of Tony's stubble.

"You kept that quiet," he murmured, breathing in Tony's scent.

Tony's chuckle rumbled through his chest. "Could say the same thing about you." He tilted Harry's head with his fingers and kissed him, chaste at first, then his tongue parted Harry's lips, and the kiss morphed into something a whole lot more sensual and intimate. Harry cupped Tony's nape, deepening the kiss, until at last they parted.

Tony gazed into his eyes. "You know that was dangerous, right? The fasting?"

Harry sighed. "Yeah. To be honest, I'd already decided to quit it. I'll look at other ways of losing weight. Less risky ones."

Tony cocked his head. "You still wanna lose weight? Are you that unhappy with how you look?"

Harry pulled free of his arms and sat back. "This is hard to explain."

"Try."

Harry clasped his hands in his lap. "You know I told you I didn't always look like this?" Tony nodded. "I started eating more when I came back to live with Mum. I know why. Guilt."

Tony frowned. "What did you have to feel guilty about?"

He stared at his clasped hands. "I'd moved out, I was living in London, enjoying myself, and meanwhile she was living her on her own. I only saw how lonely she'd become when I moved back. So yeah, I felt guilty. I wasn't thinking about her—I was only thinking of myself."

"Kids leave home, right?" Then Tony

snickered. "Well, most of the time. What I mean is, you moving out was normal. You can't kick yourself for that." He took Harry's hand in his.

"Except it got worse. When I finally did move back, I only got a couple of years with her before she died. Which made me feel even more guilty. I knew I was overdoing it, but eating became a sort of… crutch, and it only got worse when she died."

"You couldn't break the habit?"

Harry shook his head. "I'd look in the mirror and I'd think, 'No one's going to look at me, so why bother trying to look better? It'd be a pointless exercise, a useless activity." He paused and took a deep breath. "It wasn't until recently that I took a long, hard look at myself. Not just at how I looked, but how I *thought*. You know what I discovered? Nearly every word I said or thought about myself ended the same way. Pointless. Useless. Friendless." He squeezed Tony's hand. "The reason for this sudden introspection? You. I kept asking myself why you stuck around. What *you* saw in me that *I* didn't."

"I saw plenty," Tony said, his eyes shining. "A warm, generous man who made me feel good when I was around him. A caring man, who sat on the couch with me, rubbing hand cream into my callouses. Only a little thing, I know, but… it touched me. And the more time I spent with you, the more I liked what I saw. The only thing I *didn't* understand was why you were so down on yourself. Well, I guess I understand that a bit better now." He lifted Harry's hand and brought it to his lips, kissing his fingers. "You know my feelings on your appearance, but there's nothing wrong with eating healthily and doing a little exercise. Having said that, the way we're going, you're gonna be changing shape rapidly."

"What do you mean?"

Tony cackled. "Sex burns off a whole load of calories, babe. And seeing as I can't keep my mitts off ya…"

Harry laughed. "Yeah, I get that. Well, I *am* irresistible, right?"

He got two seconds before Tony swatted him with a cushion. "Okay, Mr. Irresistible. What are we gonna do about dinner? Because I'll bet the last decent meal you ate was that fish and chips with me."

Harry wasn't about to corroborate that. "How about Italian?"

Tony gave a slow nod. "Only if we go to Bagatti's. You an' me on a date. Never mind it's a weekday, I wanna take you out for dinner."

Harry couldn't think of a better way to end the day. "I'd love to. On one condition."

Tony gazed at him inquiringly. "And that is?"

"You don't go home after. Stay the night."

Tony's smiled reached his eyes. "I'd love to."

Harry groaned. "Dessert? Are you kidding?"

Tony tapped the menu. "But look. There's a warm *Panettone* and butter pudding. Profiteroles. Lemon ice cream. *Tiramisu.* Surely there's one of them that's calling to you." He knew Harry would cave eventually, especially after he'd admitted wanting sweet stuff all day.

"Fine." Harry glanced at the menu. "I'll have the *pannacotta*. Happy now?"

"Only if it comes with two spoons," Tony said with a wink.

Harry laughed. "Yeah, I can live with that."

When the waiter had taken their order for dessert and coffee, Tony sat back and patted his belly. "That was delicious." What had overjoyed him was to see Harry clearly enjoying every mouthful of his fillet steak in a red wine and dolcelatte sauce.

"Agreed." Harry raised his wine glass. "To a wonderful evening."

Tony clinked his glass against Harry's. "No argument from me." He finished the remnants of his wine and let out a happy sigh. The evening might have begun in panic, but he could never have foreseen this.

He loves me. There were no sweeter words in the entire universe.

"Actually, there was something I wanted to mention." Harry put down his glass and reached across the table for Tony's hand. "I have a… proposal to make."

Tony covered his hand with his heart. "I may faint. This is a bit sudden." To his surprise, his light-hearted tone didn't have the result he'd expected. Harry stilled, and Tony's stomach clenched. "Oh God. You weren't really about to—"

"God, no." Harry gave him a hard stare. "I think five weeks is a bit premature, don't you? Not that I'm ruling it out entirely, okay? But hell, not after five weeks."

Tony wiped his brow in mock relief, and then Harry's words fully registered. *He's not ruling it out?* The knowledge filled him with quiet joy. *He wants to marry me.*

For that, Tony would wait as long as it took.

"Then I'm intrigued. What exactly were you gonna propose?"

Harry cleared his throat, then reached for his water glass. "Well, I've been thinking—"

"Now I'm really worried."

Harry narrowed his gaze. "Bastard," he muttered. "Let me finish, why don't you?" He took another sip of water. "I have a solution to your present circumstances."

Tony was about to ask him to clarify what particular circumstances, when Harry blew him away.

"Move in with me."

He blinked. Blinked again.

Harry nodded slowly, his gaze never leaving Tony's face. "It makes sense. I have that house all to myself. You're living with your mum. So... move in with me, and we'll make it our home. You can do what the hell you like to it, because it will be *your* place too." He paused. "How does that sound?"

Tony didn't know where to begin. "I didn't think you could've topped today," he said after a moment. "I mean, seriously. Hearing you say you love me was... But now?" Then his eyes lit up. "I can do *anything* I like to it?"

"Oh hell. What have I started?"

Whatever else he'd been about to say was lost as the waiter approached with their dessert. Once he'd left them, Harry peered at Tony. "I take it that's a yes, then."

Tony couldn't stop smiling. "Too right. When can I move in?"

"As soon as you like." Harry was smiling too. "You can rope Tanya and Rocco in to help you move out." A frown creased his forehead. "You don't think… your mum will be lonely if you leave?"

Tony snorted. "Are you kidding me? She'll have my Aunt Marisa moved into my room before you blink." He picked up one of the spoons and dipped it into the rich, creamy *pannacotta*, before holding it out to Harry. "Open wide."

Harry collapsed into laughter. "I'm sorry. It's just that I was thinking about the last time you said—"

Tony rolled his eyes. "You've got a one-track mind, d'you know that? And I bleedin' love ya for it." He paused, growing serious for a moment. "I do love you, y'know."

"I know. Love you too." And there was that glow again, the one that told him Harry was happy.

Tony was determined to keep him that way.

Chapter Twenty-Five

Tony paid the taxi driver, and they walked up the tiled front path that led to the door. Harry paused a few feet away, and before he could say a word, Tony's hand was on his back, Tony's breath tickling his ear as he whispered, "You are gonna be fine. You look amazing." He nuzzled Harry's neck, making him shiver. "You smell wonderful."

Harry had to chuckle at that. "As long as you're the only one who gets this close to find that out."

"I'll be right there. And my friends are gonna love ya." Tony kissed his cheek. "Just like I love ya."

That familiar warmth that had flooded through him every time Tony said those words was back, spreading throughout his body. "Love you too."

"Then let's get in there and have a good time, okay?"

Harry drew in a deep breath. "Yeah, let's do this." Another breath.

"Harry?" Tony snickered. "You have to move your feet if we're gonna reach the front door, babe."

Harry took hold of his hand. "I just… don't want to let you down. Not in front of your friends."

Tony locked gazes with him, his face suddenly grave. "There is no way you could ever do that." He bit his lip. "Unless you get rat-arsed and end up trying to shag the dog on the patio. That might raise a few eyebrows. Relax. That's not gonna happen. Know why?" He grinned. "They haven't got a dog."

Harry snickered. Tony's joking had done the trick, however, and his nervousness dissipated a little. "I'm ready."

Tony gave him an encouraging smile, squeezed his hand, and rang the doorbell. From inside came the sound of music, and the air already carried the scent of burning charcoal. The door opened, and a guy possibly in his thirties stood there, dressed in long shorts and an apron bearing a hand pointing downward and the slogan, 'May I suggest the sausage?' His face widened into a huge grin when he saw Tony.

"Mate. I thought you were never gonna get here." His gaze flickered to Harry, and he gave him a genuine smile. "You must be Harry. Please to meet ya. I'm Dezza. Come on in."

They stepped into the house, and once the door closed behind them, Tony handed Dezza the plastic bag he'd brought with them. "Thought this might come in handy."

Dezza peered into the bag. "Oh, you're a lifesaver. We've got bottles of Lambrini comin' out of our ears in the kitchen." He caught Harry's gaze and grimaced. "Sweet white wine. *Really* not me. But some of 'em like it, thank God." He winked. "If there's any left by tonight, they can take it home with 'em too."

"Well, I remembered those nights when we used to get hammered on a bottle of Jack Daniels. Thought it would bring back memories."

Dezza arched his eyebrows. "If it's memories you want, that's what you're gonna get. You're not the only one here with a new fella. Rory's brought his—and it's someone we know." He smirked. "Yep, this is gonna be a walk down Memory Lane tonight." He turned on his heel and walked toward the rear of the house. "Follow me, boys. Everyone's in the back garden."

Harry followed Tony, leaning close. "How do you know Dezza?"

"I met him years ago in a bar in Soho. Good lad. We've been friends ever since. His parties are legend, especially when the police turn up 'cause some old biddy has complained about the noise."

They went through French doors onto a large tiled patio, where a double grill had been set up, along with a table full of burger buns, piles of cheese slices, bowls of different salads, and several bottles of condiments. Another table had every inch of its surface covered with bottles of alcohol and soft drinks. On the patio were about twenty or so guests, and there were more beyond them on the lawn, standing around and chatting, the air redolent with mouth-watering aromas. Music played from inside the house, spilling out of the doors and open windows. The temperature was perfect, and there wasn't a cloud in the late afternoon sky.

Harry gazed around him. The vast majority of guests were male, with maybe seven or eight women. Everyone seemed in a good mood, smiling and laughing, and something of the relaxed atmosphere seeped into him.

Tony was right. This was a good idea.

A tall man with a full, thick beard strode toward them, smiling. "Tony! Been way too long,

you tosser. Good to see you." He grabbed Tony in a
fierce hug, before releasing him and extending a
hand to Harry. "Glad you could join us. I'm Eric,
Dezza's better half."

"I heard that, you bitch!" Dezza called from
several feet away.

Eric grinned. "You were supposed to, you
old queen." He gazed affectionately at Dezza. "Ears
like a shit-house rat, that one." He gestured to the
drinks table. "Help yourselves, guys. There's plenty
of choice." He lowered his voice. "Especially if you
like sweet white wine." He shuddered.

Tony leaned closer and said conspiratorially,
"Dezza has a bottle of Jack you might want to try."

Eric's eyes widened. "Shit. I'd better get in
there, or that bitch will drink the lot." He kissed
Tony on the cheek. "Nice thought, babe." He left
them, heading determinedly in Dezza's direction.

"I like your friends," Harry murmured.

Tony nodded in agreement. "Those two have
been together since the earth was cooling. Or a
helluva long time in gay years, if you wanna put it
that way." He glanced around at the guests and
broke into a smile when he caught sight of a
muscular guy striding toward them, beaming.

"Love the shirt," he called out.

"It's great, innit?" Across his broad chest
were emblazoned the words, Straight But Not
Narrow. He held out a hand to Harry. "Hi. I'm Ben. I
have the misfortune to work with his majesty 'ere.
And I am delighted to finally meet ya."

"Ben." Harry could have sworn there was a
hint of warning in Tony's voice.

Ben appeared to totally ignore him. "Just got
the record, I ain't gay. I like to think of meself as

straight but enlightened." Tony snorted, and Ben regarded him mildly. "Well, I am. I 'ave to be, the stuff that *you* come out with sometimes. I mean, talk about gettin' an education." Ben cocked his head in Tony's direction. "Of course, lately, it's all been 'Arry, this, or 'Arry that."

"Ben." The warning note was stronger.

Ben's eyes gleamed with mischief. "Lookin' a little worried there, Tone. Can't think why." He was still holding Harry's hand, which he shook vigorously. "Can I just say thanks while I've got the chance, 'cause I doubt this git will let me get within five feet of ya, once I've said me piece."

"Okay, you can stop right there," Tony said, narrowing his gaze.

Ben waved his hand dismissively. "And you can shut your cakehole till I'm done, princess." He grinned at Harry, who was starting to enjoy the conversation. Unlike Tony.

"Thanks for what?" Harry asked.

"For agreeing to go out with this wanker. You 'ave *no idea* what I've had to put up with since he gave you his number. He was bleedin' miserable. Then when you finally said yes, I 'ad to put up with is moods. 'Does he like me? Is it gonna work?' Christ, it was like working with a cross between a teenage girl and a lovesick puppy day in, day out."

Tony's eyes bulged. "I did *not* say anything like that!" He turned to Harry. "Don't listen to this tosser, he's exaggerating."

Ben's eyes gleamed. "Proper pinin' he was."

"Pining? How interesting." Harry glanced at Tony, who was glaring at Ben.

Tony groaned. "I am gonna swing for you come Monday."

Ben snickered. "That's if you can catch me." He winked at Harry. "That tool belt of his weighs him down."

"Did you come here on your own this evening, or should I be commiserating with some unfortunate female?" Tony asked with a smirk.

"I was gonna bring the girlfriend, but she wanted to stop in tonight." Ben appeared puzzled. "Said she was gonna watch recordings of Strictly. I mean, who does that?"

There was a moment's pause. Tony bit his lip. "I'm sure there are lots of people who do that." He studiously avoided Harry's gaze.

"Yeah, but she wants to watch some rugby player on it. Ben someone."

"Not a fan of Strictly, then?" Harry asked him, trying not to laugh. It was bloody difficult, especially when Tony's gaze finally met his.

"Nah. I'd rather go down the pub with me mates. Watching celebrities prance about in costumes? Not my cuppa tea." Ben patted Harry on the shoulder. "Well, like I said, it's good to finally meet ya. Keep an eye on Princess 'ere. He gets a few beers inside him, and then he's up on the tables, stripping." He flashed Harry a grin. "Just 'ave your phone 'andy." And with that he sauntered off toward the food.

Tony stared after him. "Do not believe a word that man says."

Harry thought his reaction was adorable. "It's obvious he cares about you." He snickered. "Stripping, eh?"

Tony gave him an icy stare. "I have _never_ stripped in public. Well… maybe once… but—" Suddenly he froze, gaping over Harry's shoulder.

"Bloody 'ell." A warm smile spread over his face. "What are *you* doin' 'ere?"

Harry turned to see who was being addressed. A guy with reddish-blond hair and brown eyes walked toward Tony, his arms wide. "Get over here." He seized Tony in a hug, their cheeks pressed together. "God, it's great to see you. I had no idea you'd be here." He released Tony and took a step back, studying him. "You're looking well."

"Thanks. You too." Tony turned to Harry, putting his arm around his waist. "This is my boyfriend, Harry."

Just hearing Tony say the words made Harry glow inside.

The guy regarded Harry with interest. "It's good to meet you, Harry. I'm Stu. Tony and me go way back."

Tony coughed. "That's an understatement. Anyway, how come you're here? You don't normally come to these shindigs."

Stu incline his head to the rear of the garden. "I'm here with Rory. He's my new fella. When he said he was taking me to a party, I had no idea it was Dezza's and Eric's." He regarded Tony warmly. "It's been a few years. You still look gorgeous."

"Flatterer."

"Hey, Stu? What does a guy have to do to get a drink around here?" A loud voice called out.

Stu flushed. "Oops. I was supposed to be getting Rory a drink, but I keep stopping to talk to all these familiar faces. I'd better get him one." He left them and went to the drinks table.

Harry wasn't sure how to feel about these undoubtedly good-looking men who were clearly delighted to see Tony. "You seem very... popular."

Tony cocked his head to one side. "That doesn't bother you, does it? Because the way *I* see it, you just got yourself a whole new load of friends." He flung out his arm to encompass the long garden. "There are people here I've known for years. Good people, who'd do anything for a mate. And if you wanted to find yourself new friends, you couldn't be in a better place." He faced Harry, leaned in, and kissed him slowly on the lips. "Let them get to know ya, babe. This is a safe place."

Harry drew in a deep breath. "I'm sorry. It's just that…"

"It's okay, I get it. Your world has shrunk since your mum died. Well, it's time to expand it again." He took Harry's hand. "And I'll be right here with ya." Suddenly he grimaced. "That is, when I get back from the loo. Shouldn't have drunk all that coffee today." And with that, he made a dash into the house.

Harry laughed. He was getting used to Tony waking up in the middle of the night to use the bathroom. When he got back into bed, what followed was more cuddles.

Dezza appeared at his side. "Has that man of yours not got you a drink yet?" He shook his head. "What would you like?"

"A beer would be great."

Dezza beamed. "That, I can do." He returned a minute later with an opened bottle. "There ya go."

Harry thanked him and took a long drink from it, relishing its icy trickle down his throat.

"I see Stu came over."

Harry nodded. "He seemed very happy to see Tony here."

Dezza's gaze followed the path Stu had

taken. "Yeah, those two parted on really good terms."

Harry frowned. "I don't understand."

"Stu and Tony. They dated, oh, about three years ago. Mind you, they've known each other for a damn sight longer than that."

"Dezza! We need more sausages," Eric called out.

"Coming, my love!" Dezza rolled his eyes. "Gotta keep the cook sweet, right?" He headed into the house.

Harry stared after him. *Stu is Tony's ex*? He wasn't sure how this made him feel. He had no time to process the information, before he saw Stu walking over to him, a bottle in his hand.

"So, you and Tony. How long have you been dating?" he asked pleasantly.

"Just over a month."

Stu gave a frank smile. "Well, it doesn't take a genius to see he's happy. I'm glad."

Harry couldn't hold back the words. "Why did you and he break up?"

Stu sighed. "It wasn't as if we were together all that long. Maybe three months at the most? We were better as friends than lovers. I think we both knew that. We weren't what the other needed, I suppose." He took a drink from his bottle. "Tony's a great guy. And when he's in a relationship, he invests himself totally."

"Yeah, I can see that."

Stu studied him carefully. "I think you really do. Maybe you're just what he needs, too. He always did have a thing for bears." He looked Harry up and down. "In fact, you're probably perfect for him. Where did he find you? The Build-a-Bear Factory?"

Harry chuckled. "His first attempt at getting my attention? Wolf whistles from the site where he's working."

Stu snorted. "Oh my God, that is *so* Tony."

"Are you sharing horror stories with my boyfriend?" Tony joined them, grinning.

"Not trying to scare him off, I swear." Stu gave Harry a warm smile. "Good to talk to you."

"You too." Harry watched as Stu picked his way through the guests, to where a slim man waited on the lawn. The two men kissed, before strolling down the garden, their arms around each other.

"About Stu. He's—"

"Your ex? Yeah, I know." Harry took another drink of beer. "Seems like a nice bloke." Tony arched his eyebrows, and Harry frowned. "What?"

Tony regarded him incredulously. "You continually surprise me, you know that? I thought you'd have felt… I don't know… uncomfortable? Threatened?"

Harry was puzzled. "Why should I feel threatened or uncomfortable? I'm the one who's here with you. And I'm going to be the one who'll be here with you at these parties for a long time to come." He kissed Tony on the mouth, then looked him in the eye. "Besides, I've got nothing to worry about."

"Oh? How'd you make that out?" Tony appeared amused by the statement.

Harry gestured to the assembled guests. "All these guys, and not one bear in sight. I've got it made."

Tony laughed. "Fuckin' 'ell. Is my Harry finally embracing his beardom?"

"He might be?" Harry kissed him again. "But *I* might be looking around for a new fella if you don't fetch me a burger. I'm starving."

Tony was still laughing as he went off in search of food.

Harry finished his beer and set the bottle down in a nearby plastic bowl already half-full of empties. He watched Tony laughing and chatting with guys around the food table, watched how Eric threatened to skewer him with the barbecue fork, and smiled to himself.

Life was good.

Chapter Twenty-Six

Tony stretched and rolled onto his side, reaching for Harry—who wasn't there. When he heard noises from the kitchen, he sighed with contentment. *Aw.* Already the aroma of freshly brewed coffee percolated its way up the stairs. He lay on his back, hands behind his head, thoroughly rested and content.

The party had been a blast. They were both more than a little tipsy by the time they climbed out of the taxi, and that was entirely due to Dezza insisting they 'help' him drink the Jack Daniels. Of course, Eric had got in on the act, and the rest was history. Tony was still marvelling at how relaxed Harry had seemed. Not only that, Tony's friends had really taken to him, and there had been invitations to more parties, which Harry appeared more than happy to accept.

His friends' approval wasn't a deal breaker as far as Tony was concerned, but the knowledge that they liked his partner only added to his belief that Harry was the one for him.

Tony suddenly became aware that the sheet was moving. A little lump rippled its way toward him. He laughed and lifted the sheet to reveal Star. "Good morning, cutie. And how did you get under there?" He scooped her up and settled her on top of the sheet. "No offence, kitty, but there are bits under there that don't react well to claws, and I'd like to keep 'em intact, thank you very much."

Star gave her customary yawn, and curled up next to him, while he scritched her behind the ears. It wasn't long before her motorboat purr was evident.

"What are you thinking about? You look miles away." Harry carried a tray into the bedroom, and Tony sniffed the air. "Yeah, your favourite— hot, buttered toast and coffee." What was comical was that Star's nose twitched too.

Tony loved the fact that Harry was naked, whereas before he'd have put on shorts to walk around the house. *He's certainly loosened up a lot.*

He sat up in bed and stuffed pillows behind him. "You spoil me. Do I get this every morning?" With one hand he lazily stroked Star's back. *I could get used to this.*

Harry snickered. "You saw me on Friday morning, right? I usually leave things to the last minute, then end up hurrying for the bus. You might get a mug of coffee waiting for you in the kitchen." His face lit up. "Hey. We can travel together, seeing as we're both going to the same place."

Shit. Tony knew he'd forgotten something. "Yeah, about that. There's something I need to tell ya."

Harry set down the tray on the bedside cabinet. "Something important?"

"Well… we finished work on the site on Friday."

Harry sat on the edge of the bed. "Really? Have you got another job lined up?"

Tony nodded. "We start on a big new development in Epsom on Monday." He watched Harry's cheerful expression falter. "Hey, what's wrong?"

"Oh, nothing much, I suppose." Harry

depressed the plunger on the cafetière and filled the mugs with coffee. "It's just that I've sort of got used to seeing you every morning. Having you waiting for me every evening. I'll miss that."

Tony laughed. "Idiot. You're gonna be waking up next to me every morning, or had you forgotten that part? And I'll be the last thing you see every night." All of which was just perfect in Tony's book.

Harry's eyes lit up. "You're right. I'm an idiot. And speaking of which… when do you think you'll move in?"

"I don't wanna hang about," Tony admitted. He didn't want to waste a minute of being with Harry.

"Do you have much stuff to bring here?"

He gave a gleeful smile. "A *lot* of stuff. It might take two or three trips with the truck."

Harry poured milk into the mugs, then handed him one. "Which brings me to my next point. Where is it all going to fit?"

Tony had been thinking about that. He put down his mug, threw back the sheet, and got out of bed. "Come with me," he said, taking Harry by the hand. He led him out of the room and next door into the smallest bedroom. There was no bed, but stacks and stacks of cardboard boxes, taking up all the floor space. "What's in these?"

"Things that belonged to my parents."

Tony had figured as much. "I was thinking, this would make a good-sized dressing room. I could build fitted wardrobes along one wall, a chest of drawers at that end, then put up a full-length mirror. That would give us more space in our room."

Harry's face glowed. "I love that you said

our room."

Tony kissed him on the nose. "Well, it will be, right?"

"I already think of it as ours."

Tony loved that.

He led Harry to the rear bedroom, yet another room full of boxes, although there was a bed beneath them. "More stuff belonging to your mum and dad?" When Harry nodded, Tony said nothing. He knew what he longed to suggest, but it wasn't his place to do this.

This had to be Harry's decision.

Harry peered into the room and sighed. "I think I need to go through all this."

Bless him. Tony wanted to hold him and tell him he was doing the right thing, but he was afraid it would come out wrong. "Decluttering is the in thing nowadays."

"I like your idea for a dressing room, by the way." Harry tilted his head to one side. "So what else would you do in the house?"

Tony had been thinking about that as well.

He beckoned with his finger. "Let me show you." He went down the stairs, Harry following. A thought occurred to him. "Do I need to draw the curtains in the living room?"

Harry snickered. "I've given up on that. If they want to peer in with their high-powered telescopes and binoculars, let them. We'll just give them a show. They'll either run away screaming, or we'll end up having to sell tickets." He shrugged. "Okay, so maybe I'm not *that* comfortable with it, but I'm making a real effort not to care so much about how people see me."

Tony was *really* liking this new Harry.

They entered the living room, and Tony pointed to the far end that backed onto the garden. "See that radiator under the window? I'd move it to this wall, then make the window into French doors. That way, they'd open out onto that little brick patio out there, with those steps going down into the garden."

"I like that." Harry beamed. "What else?"

"Well, there's your dad's old garage, and that old greenhouse over on the right. If we knocked those down, we'd have more space. You could build a deck out there, where we could sit out in the summer and eat. You could even hold your own parties."

"*We* could hold *our* own parties," Harry reminded him with a smirk. "This hasn't sunk in yet, has it? This is *your* home too."

"Does that mean you like my ideas?"

Harry's face glowed. "I love them."

"So, when would you like me to start all these fabulous renovations?"

Harry grinned. "When can you move in?"

"I see." Tony guffawed. "I gain a boyfriend, you gain a labourer."

Harry put his arms around him. "Hardly that. A master craftsman. A man with very talented hands." He grabbed one of them. "So why don't we go upstairs, and you can put those talented hands to good use?"

Part of Tony's anatomy really liked that idea. "Doing what? As if I couldn't guess."

Harry smirked. "Eating your toast that's going cold as we speak. Plus, there's coffee." He let go of Tony's hand and walked out of the room.

"And here was me thinking we were on the

same page."

Harry's chuckle drifted down the stairs. "That comes after the toast and coffee. Especially if you get butter on your dick. I'll have to lick it off."

Tony suddenly found a very pressing reason to go upstairs.

"And when we're finished," Harry said as Tony entered the bedroom, "I have something in mind that will probably take us the rest of the day to complete."

Tony raised his eyebrows. "Which is?"

"You're going to help me go through all those boxes. I'll decide what things I'm keeping, then the rest of it can go to the tip or the charity shops." Harry gave him a calm smile. "New start."

Tony nodded, his heart bursting with pride for his man. "New start."

Harry threw back the sheets and patted the mattress. "Now get that fine arse in here. But get crumbs in the bed, and you're a dead man."

Tony had already considered that. "No problem. I'm gonna use you for a plate, and I'll lick up any crumbs I make."

Breakfast had never promised to be so much fun. Once the furry spectator had been removed, of course.

Epilogue

One year later

Harry took the bottle of white wine from the fridge and carried it through the house and out into the garden. He went over to where Tony was busy flipping burgers on the built-in grill, laughing and chatting animatedly with some of their guests. Harry slipped behind him and leaned in to ask quietly, "Have you seen Star?"

Tony laughed. "She'll be on someone's lap. That kitty is a real attention whore."

He had a point. Star had to have received pets and cuddles from virtually every guest at the party. Their garden was full to bursting, and there were more guests inside, the sound of animated conversations drifting through the French windows.

Harry loved what Tony had done to the place. Little by little he'd transformed the dull-as-ditch water house into a beautiful, comfortable home. A space for entertaining their friends, something that was a frequent activity. He particularly loved the way the garden had become an extension of the house, with areas for sitting and enjoying the weather whenever possible.

"Hey, Tony, let me take over." Rocco appeared beside them. "You haven't had a chance to mingle all afternoon." He held out his hand. "Come on. Hand over the apron." He smirked. "So is this true, Harry?" Rocco pointed to where the words Caution - Hot Stuff stood out in red on the apron's black background.

Harry grinned. "A gentleman never tells."

Tony snorted. "Well, that lets you out." Harry gave him a mock glare, and Tony responded by blowing him a kiss. "Thanks, Rocco. I appreciate this. Just make sure the burgers end up in the buns and not in your belly. I know what you're like around barbecue."

"It's a vicious rumour, spread by your sister."

Tony laughed. "Yeah, yeah, 'course it is." He grabbed Harry's hand. "Come on, let's mingle." He peered down. "Why are you carrying a bottle of white wine?"

Harry gave him a sweet smile. "Because your mum asked if there was any, that's why. So let me get this to her, and then we can chat with our guests." He was delighted so many had turned up to their last party of the summer, especially because this one promised to be fantastic.

I hope.

"Have I told you yet how sexy you look in these new jeans?" Tony's hand strayed to his arse and gave it a quick squeeze. "Especially this part. And before you complain that everyone will see, let me remind you. Me fondling your arse will not come as a shock to a single one of our guests."

He had a point. Harry coughed slightly. "Fair enough, but don't give your mum more ammunition."

Tony instantly removed his hand as they approached his mum. "Wine, Mamá?"

She smiled as Harry held out the bottle for her. "You're a good lad." She grinned when he filled her glass to the brim. "A *very* good lad."

"You having a good time, Mamá?"

She nodded, squeezing Tony's arm. "I've been talking with those two men over there. Such a lovely couple." Glass in hand, she pointed to where Dezza and Eric stood by the garden fence, deep in conversation with Tanya. "They're giving her ideas for her and Rocco's next holiday."

Eric worked in a travel agent's, and he'd been the one who'd sorted out all the details for their upcoming holiday. Harry couldn't wait.

"The one with the beard. He said something about you and Tony going to Spain next week, but I think he got it wrong. He kept mentioning bears."

Tony coughed loudly, and Harry patted his back. "You all right there, babe?"

"We'll be back in a bit, Mamá." Tony grabbed Harry by the arm and led him away. He leaned closer and hissed, "I am *not* about to explain to my mum what Bear Week is."

Harry smirked. "I don't think it would faze her in the slightest. And speaking of Spain… I'm glad you appreciate the new jeans, because you know exactly where I bought them, right?"

Tony laughed. "And how is Arnold?"

Harry had gone into Arnold's shop to buy some new clothes for the trip. "More excitable than usual. Guess who else is going to Sitges next week?"

Tony raised his eyes heavenward. "Oh God. Arnold loose in a sea of bears. Heaven help 'em."

The shop where Arnold worked had become Harry's go-to place when it came to clothes shopping, and during the last year, he'd become friends with the exuberant shop assistant. "I said we'll meet him for a drink at some point."

Tony snorted again. "If he isn't curled up in some bear's lap." He glanced over Harry's shoulder and waved. "Stu and Rory are here."

"Great!" He turned and waved too. "Help yourselves to drinks, guys. We'll be over in a minute." Harry had gotten to know them really well. They often came around for dinner, and Harry had to admit, he felt extremely comfortable with them.

Tony was right. That party opened the doors to a lot of new friendships.

"Aw, isn't she adorable?" Deb's voice rose above the chatter, and Harry chuckled.

"Star claims another heart."

Tony pulled him close. "Not difficult, when she's easily as lovable as her daddy."

"So you still love me then?" Harry teased.

"With all my heart." Tony kissed him softly.

"Get a room," came a voice from behind them. Harry broke free of Tony's arms and turned to find Simon grinning at him. "Evening, boss." At his side was Dan, his boyfriend of the last three months. "So, are you packed yet?"

Tony snickered. "He was packed a week ago."

"There's nothing wrong with being prepared," Harry remonstrated. "Just because *you* leave everything to the last minute." It was strange how living with Tony had changed his habits. Their roles appeared to have reversed, and it was Harry who was up with the lark, making breakfast for them. He had an ulterior motive, of course.

He wanted to spend as much time as possible with Tony.

Harry slipped his hand into his pocket, checking for the umpteenth time. Yup. Still there.

"Do you think everyone is here now?"

Tony laughed. "Babe, if they're not, we need a bigger garden."

Harry's heartbeat sped up. No time like the present. "Excuse me a sec." He climbed up onto a nearby garden wall that surrounded one of the raised flower beds. "If I can have everyone's attention? Those of you indoors, could you come out here please?"

Tony gave him an inquiring glance. "Need a loudhailer?"

Harry ignored him. The conversations died as their guests stood still, their faces turned toward him.

Here goes.

"First of all, Tony and I would like to thank you all for coming to our last party of the summer. There have been a few, and some of you were here for all of them." He stared at Dezza and Eric. "And yes, I mean you two." Laughter broke out.

Tony came up to him. "Don't talk for too long, or Rocco will burn the sausages again."

"I heard that!" More laughter ensued.

Harry cleared his throat. "As some of you know, next week, Tony and I are off to sunny Spain—"

"Yeah, bear watching!" Stu called out, grinning.

"I don't need to go bear watching," Tony retorted, before beaming proudly at them. "I'm taking mine with me."

Harry gave him a fond smile. "And to everyone else who wonders what the hell we're talking about, Tony will be pleased to explain it to you later." A ripple of chuckles ran through the assembled guests, accompanied by a few snorts and guffaws. "I'm really looking forward to this holiday. I've been excited about it, ever since I realized that it was going to be a holiday with a difference."

Tony raised his eyebrows but said nothing.

Harry got down off the wall and stood in front of Tony. "You see, I was sort of hoping that it would be our… honeymoon." He removed the box from his pocket and opened it.

Tony's jaw dropped. "I don't fuckin' believe it," he muttered.

Harry blinked. "Not quite the reaction I was hoping for." His breathing quickened. "I take it you didn't expect this."

Tony shook his head. "You don't get it." He reached into his pocket and pulled out a box. A very similar box.

"You have got to be kidding me!" Harry stared as Tony opened it to reveal a white gold band.

A very similar ring.

Beside them, Simon spoke. "As if we needed more proof that you two are meant to be together."

Harry barely registered the words. He gazed at the two rings, amazed.

"You beat me to it," Tony said at last. "So I guess you know what the answer's gonna be, right?" Around them came *aws* and murmured approval.

"Well, will *one* of you answer at least?" Tony's mum's exasperated tone broke through. "Is it a yes?"

Harry locked gazes with Tony, and with one voice they said, "Yes." A second later they were in each other's arms, their lips locked in a kiss. Harry's heart was pounding, and he thought it might burst with sheer joy. They'd both known this day would come, but to realize they were so in tune with one another made Harry's heart sing.

Applause broke out, and they were surrounded by friends patting them on the back and sharing their congratulations. Harry didn't see them—he only had eyes for Tony.

Tanya, Rocco and Dezza made sure everyone's glass was filled, and then Stu proposed a toast, wishing them every happiness. Harry waited until all the fuss had died down before leading Tony into the house.

"I wanted this bit to be just us," he explained, taking Tony's hand and sliding the ring onto his finger. He sighed with happiness as Tony did the same. "I still can't believe we both got rings."

"That's 'cause Simon's right. We're meant to be together." Tony cupped Harry's nape with one hand, and with the other he stroked his beard. He drew Harry into a kiss that send a surge of peace flowing through him.

Meant to be. Harry felt that, with all his heart.

"I love you," he murmured. "More than I did before, yet not as much as I will do in the years to come."

Tony stilled. "That was beautiful. Almost as beautiful as you. Love you too." He sighed. "I love the idea of next week being our honeymoon, but you know we can't get married before then, right?"

"I know." Harry kissed him softly. "It was a lovely idea though."

"So here's what we do. We treat it as a trial honeymoon, then we get to do it all over again once it's legal." He grinned. "For now, you just claimed me, that's all."

Harry arched his eyebrows. "*Claimed* you?"

Tony smiled. "Isn't that what bears do?"

"Hey, you two! Enough time for canoodlin' when all the guests have gone. There's a party goin' on out 'ere, in case you 'aven't noticed."

Tony rolled his eyes. "Thanks, Ben, yeah. We were aware of that." He took Harry's hand. "Come on. Let's go celebrate with our friends."

Harry kissed him on the mouth. "As long as I get to celebrate with you later. Just us."

Tony's eyes sparkled. "Absofuckinglutely."

The End

A message from K.C.

Thank you for purchasing this copy of Denim. It's been a fun–and sometimes painful–journey with Harry and Tony, and my apologies to all of you who messaged to find out when it was being released.

I didn't want to rush this one.

If you've enjoyed Denim, please consider leaving a review, however brief, on Amazon. Reviews are what make books visible, and without them, we struggle. And if there are aspects of the book that you feel hindered your enjoyment, then share those too. How else are we to grow as writers? No author minds receiving an honest, constructive critique.

This time I don't have an extract from the next book in the series, for the simple reason that I've not yet decided which one will be next. But to give you a hint of what's to come, there are at least three more: Leather, Suede and Skin. Although I've been much amused by some readers' suggestions for possible titles. Cotton, Polyester and Pleather will **not** be among them.

Thanks for your support. On the following pages are details of upcoming books, both from Dreamspinner Press and my self-published titles. This year marks a new departure for me – my first murder mystery!

I can't wait to share all these new stories with you.

Take care of yourselves, and keep reading!

KCWells

Coming soon from Dreamspinner Press

August, 2018

<u>Threepeat</u> (Book #3 in the <u>Secrets</u> series, written with Parker Williams.)

Can two Doms open their hearts again for a young man desperately in need of their help?

Two years ago, Aaron Greene and Sam Thompson were devastated when their submissive broke the contract that bound the three of them together. They still wonder what happened and whether they can find a way to move forward. When Aaron finds a sick young man by the curbside, his protective instincts kick in, and after consulting Sam, he takes Tim home.

After being thrown out of his home, Tim Waterman finds himself on the street, doing whatever he needed to survive. Until a bear of a Good Samaritan scoops him up and saves him. Then one bear becomes two, and a chance discovery gets him thinking about what might be, if he's bold enough to make a move.

So what happens when Aaron and Sam wake up one morning to find Tim naked in their bed? Will they get a new chance at life, or will history Threepeat itself?

October, 2018.

Truth Will Out (A Merrychurch Mystery)

Jonathon de Mountford's visit to Merrychurch village to stay with his uncle Dominic gets off to a bad start when Dominic fails to appear at the railway station. But when Jonathon finds him dead in his study, apparently as the result of a fall, everything changes. For one thing, Jonathon is the next in line to inherit the manor house. For another, he's not so sure it was an accident, and with the help of Mike Tattersall, the owner of the village pub, Jonathon sets out to prove his theory—if he can concentrate long enough, without getting distracted by the handsome Mike.

They discover an increasingly long list of people who had reason to want Dominic dead. And when events take an unexpected turn, the amateur sleuths are left bewildered. It doesn't help that the police inspector brought in to solve the case is the last person Mike wants to see, especially when they are told to keep their noses out of police business.

In Jonathon's case, that's like a red rag to a bull….

DENIM

Coming soon from *K.C. Wells*

<u>Truth & Betrayal</u>

All the light went out of Jake's life when his older brother Caleb died in a traffic accident. Getting through the aftermath was always going to be the hardest thing he'd ever done, but finding out that the tall stranger at the graveside was the one driving the car? At least Jake now has a target for all the rage inside him. Because the man responsible for stealing Caleb's light from the world has no right to intrude on their grief.

Liam had known deep down that it was a mistake to go to Tennessee, but he'd hoped saying goodbye to Caleb would ease the pain inside him. The hostile reception from Caleb's family was no surprise, but it galled him the way they claimed ownership of him, like they knew everything about Caleb. Liam knows the truth—they had no clue about Caleb's life, and maybe it was better that way. Caleb's secrets would die with him.

When Jake turns up at Caleb's apartment in Atlanta to collect his brother's possessions, the last person he expects to see is Liam. And there are more revelations to come, knowledge that will turn Jake's world upside down, bringing with it yet more pain and anguish.

Two men hurting. Two men seeking comfort - and finding it where they least expect it.

Available Titles

By K.C. Wells

<u>Learning to Love</u>
Michael & Sean
Evan & Daniel
Josh & Chris
Final Exam

Love Lessons Learned
A Bond of Three
Le lien des Trois
A Bond of Truth
First
Debt
Dette
Il Debito
Schuld
Waiting for You
The Senator's Secret
Out of the Shadows
Step by Step
Pas à Pas
BFF

<u>Collars & Cuffs</u>
An Unlocked Heart
Trusting Thomas
Someone to Keep Me
(K.C. Wells & Parker Williams)
A Dance with Domination
Damian's Discipline
(K.C. Wells & Parker Williams)

DENIM

Make Me Soar
Dom of Ages
(K.C. Wells & Parker Williams)
Endings and Beginnings
(K.C. Wells & Parker Williams)

Un Coeur Déverrouillé
Croire en Thomas
Te Protéger

Secrets – with Parker Williams
Before You Break
An Unlocked Mind

Personal
Making it Personal
Personal Changes
More than Personal
Personal Secrets
Strictly Personal
Personal Challenges

Une Affaire Personnelle
Changements Personnels
Plus Personnel
Secrets Personnels
Strictement Personnel

Una Questione Personale
Cambiamenti Personali
Piú che personale
Segreti Personali
Strettamente personale

𝒦.𝒞. 𝒲𝐸𝐿𝐿𝒮

Es wird persönlich
Persönliche Veränderungen
Mehr als Persönliche
Persönliche Geheimnisse
Streng Persönlich

Confetti, Cake & Confessions
Confetti, Coriandoli e Confessioni

Connections
Connexion

Saving Jason
Per Salvare Jason
Jasons Befreiung
A Christmas Promise

Island Tales
Waiting for a Prince
September's Tide
Submitting to the Darkness

Le Maree di Settembre
In Attesa di un Principe

Lightning Tales
Teach Me
Trust Me
See me
Love Me

Lehre Mich
Vertau Mir
Sieh Mich

DENIM

Liebe Mich

Il Professore
Fidati di me

A Material World
Lace
Satin
Silk

Spitze
Satin
Seide

Pizzo

Double or Nothing
Back from the Edge
Switching it up
Scambio di ruoli

Anthologies

Fifty Gays of Shade
Winning Will's Heart

About the author

K.C. Wells started writing in 2012, although the idea of writing a novel had been in her head since she was a child. But after reading that first gay romance in 2009, she was hooked.

She now writes full time, and the line of men in her head, clamouring to tell their story, is getting longer and longer. If the frequent visits by plot bunnies are anything to go by, that's not about to change anytime soon.

If you want to follow her exploits, you can sign up for her monthly newsletter: http://eepurl.com/cNKHlT

You can stalk – er, find – her in the following places:
Facebook:
https://www.facebook.com/KCWellsWorld

https://www.facebook.com/kcwells.WildWickedWonderful/
Goodreads:
https://www.goodreads.com/author/show/6576876.K_C_Wells
Instagram: **https://www.instagram.com/k.c.wells/**
Twitter: **https://twitter.com/K_C_Wells**
Blog: **http://kcwellsworld.blogspot.co.uk/**
Website: **http://www.kcwellsworld.com/**

Alter Egos

Writing MF romance as Kathryn Greenway

Kathryn Greenway lives on the Isle of Wight, off the southern coast of the UK, in a typical English village where there are few secrets, and everyone knows everyone else.

She writes romance in different genres, and under different pen names, but her goal is always the same - to reach that Happily Ever After.

Pulled by a Dream is Kathryn's debut novel, although in a whole other life, she is K.C. Wells, a bestselling author of gay romance.

Website: **https://www.kathryngreenway.com/**
Facebook: **https://www.facebook.com/KathrynGreen...**
Twitter: **https://twitter.com/KGreenwayauthor**
Instagram: **https://www.instagram.com/kgreenwayau...**
Goodreads: **https://www.goodreads.com/author/show/17633635.Kathryn_Greenway**
Amazon: **https://www.amazon.com/-/e/B0795VY3TM**

You can find Pulled by a Dream here:
http://mybook.to/PBAD

Who is Tantalus?

For those who like their stories intensely erotic, featuring hot men and even hotter sex….
Who don't mind breaking the odd taboo now and again….
Who want to read something that adds a little heat to their fantasies….
…there's Tantalus.
Because we all need a little tantalizing.
Tantalus is the hotter, more risqué alter ego of K.C. Wells
Amazon page:
https://www.amazon.com/Tantalus/e/B01IN33IZO

Playing with Fire (Damon & Pete)
A series of (so far) four short gay erotic stories:
Summer Heat
After
Consequences
Limits

(Hopefully) coming in 2018, the first Tantalus novel in a new series, Leather & Kink

DENIM

Learning the Notes

Steven Torland is about to reach his fiftieth birthday, and to celebrate the occasion, his publicist decides it's time someone wrote a biography of the famous composer and musician. When writer Kyle Mann is approached with the idea, he's flattered and leaps at the chance. It will be his first biography. The idea of spending six months getting to know Steven and researching his history excites him, but there is the added frisson that Steven is sexy as hell. Kyle has always had a thing for older men, and it's no secret that Steven is gay. In his heart Kyle knows it's just a fantasy, but he can still dream, right?

It doesn't take Steven long to realize he wants Kyle in his bed, and Steven usually gets what he wants. But Kyle proves to be more than a convenient fuck. There's something about him that leads Steven to think maybe it's time to let Kyle see the real Steven Torland, the one who is no stranger to the leather community of San Francisco. Steven aims to take things nice and slow, because he doesn't want this one to get away. He wants it all – a lover in his life and a boy in his bed – and he wants to see just how far he can push Kyle, and what Kyle is prepared to do to please him.

Kyle has no idea how much his life is about to change….

Made in the USA
Middletown, DE
27 October 2023

41510706R00156